# Welcome ıo Land of Fright™

**Land of Fright**™ is a world of spine-tingling short horror stories filled with the strange, the eerie, and the weird. The **Land of Fright**™ tales encompass the vast expanse of time and space. In the **Land of Fright™** series of books you will visit the world of the Past in Ancient Rome, Medieval England, the old West, World War II, and other eras yet to be explored. You will find many tales that exist right here in the Present, tales filled with modern lives that have taken a turn down a darker path. You will travel into the Future to tour strange new worlds and interact with alien societies, or to just take a disturbing peek at what tomorrow may bring.

Each **Land of Fright**™ story exists in its own territory (which we like to call a **terrorstory**.) These terrorstories can be visited in any order you choose. Some of the story realms you visit will intrigue you. Some of them may unsettle you. Some of them may even titillate and amuse you. We hope many of them will give you delicious chills along your journey. And there are many new uncharted realms yet to be mapped, so keep checking back for new discoveries.

First, we need to check your ID. **Land of Fright**™ is intended for mature audiences. You will experience adult language, graphic violence, and some explicit sex. Ready to enter? Good. We'll take that ticket now. **Land of Fright**™ awaits. You can pass through the dark gates and—Step Into Fear!

# Readers Love Land of Fright™!

"This is the first story I've read by this author and it blew me away! A gripping tale that kept me wondering until the end. Images from this will, I fear, haunt me at unexpected moments for many months to come. Readers, be warned! :)" – Amazon review for **Dung Beetles (Land of Fright™ #27 – in Collection III)**

"Some truly original stories. At last, a great collection of unique and different stories. Whilst this is billed as horror, the author managed to steer away from senseless violence and gratuitous gore and instead with artful story telling inspires you to use your own imagination. A great collection. Already looking for other collections… especially loved Kill the Queen (God Save the Queen)." – Amazon UK review for **Land of Fright™ Collection I**

"This was a great story. Even though it was short I still connected with the main character and was rooting for her. Once I read the twist I cheered her on. This was an enjoyable short story." – Amazon review for **Snowflakes (Land of Fright™ #3 – in Collection I)**

"Four stars. Real strange story." – Amazon UK review for **Hitler's Graveyard (Land of Fright™ #25 – in Collection III)**

"Loved the twist. A good short story with a hilarious twist. Great lunch time read." – Amazon review for **Trophy Wives (Land of Fright™ #5 – in Collection I)**

"…a good read. Well-written and entertaining." – Amazon review for **Special Announcement (Land of Fright™ #11 – in Collection II)**

"I like the idea of a malevolent dimension that finds a way to reach into our world... this was an entertaining read and can be read at lunch or as a palate cleanser between longer stories." – Amazon review for **Sparklers (Land of Fright™ #15 – in Collection II)**

"Pool of light was such a great story. It gave you just enough information to let your mind take over and it was a story you could read on your break. I liked how it wasn't a typical horror story. Would highly recommend." – Amazon review for **Pool of Light (Land of Fright™ #13 – in Collection II)**

"I enjoyed this quite a bit, but then I enjoy anything set in Pompeii. A horror story is a first, though, and well done. I'm become a fan of the author and so far have enjoyed several of his stories." – Amazon review for **Ghosts of Pompeii (Land of Fright™ #14 – in Collection II)**

"Fantastic science fiction short that has a surprising plot twist, great aliens, cool future tech and occurs in a remote lived-in future mining colony on a distant planet. This short hit all the marks I look for in science fiction stories. The alien creatures are truly alien and attack with a mindless ruthlessness. The desperate colonists defend themselves in a uniquely futuristic way. This work nails the art of the short story. Recommended." – Amazon review for **Out of Ink (Land of Fright™ #26 – in Collection III)**

"A harried corporate drone is presented with a bizarre choice when he stumbles onto the beginning of a unbelievable world changing event occurring in a hidden basement floor of his corporate office. This tale had me wondering, what would I do? This short fits right in with the theme of the entertaining and delightfully offbeat Land of Fright series: weird, unexpected, powerful and surreal short fiction. Recommended."- Amazon review for **The Tinies (Land of Fright™ #28 – in Collection III)**

"Another great story; I've become a fan of Mr. O'Donnell. Please keep them coming…" – Amazon review for **Sands of the Colosseum (Land of Fright™ #18 – in Collection II)**

"Perfect bite size weirdness. Land of Fright does it again with this Zone like short that has two creative plot twists that really caught me off guard. I know comparing this type of work to the Twilight Zone is overdone but it really is a high compliment that denotes original, well conceived and delightfully weird short fiction. Recommended." – Amazon review for **Flipbook (Land of Fright™ #19 – in Collection II)**

"An enjoyable story; refreshingly told from the point of view of the cat…definitely good suspense." – Amazon review for **Pharaoh's Cat (Land of Fright™ #30 – in Collection III)**

"An enjoyable story, as always. Well-written and keeps you wondering…." – Amazon review for **The Tinies (Land of Fright™ #28 – in Collection III)**

"This short has a cool premise and was very effective at quickly transporting me to the sands of the coliseum in ancient Rome. The images of dead and dying gladiators are detailed and vivid. There is a malevolent force that very much likes its job and is not about to give it up, ever. Recommended." – Amazon review for **Hammer of Charon (Land of Fright™ #29 – in Collection III)**

"The thing I like about the Land of Fright series of short stories is that they are so diverse yet share a common weird, unusual and original vibe. From horror to science fiction they are all powerful despite of their brevity. Another great addition to the Land of Fright festival of the odd." - Amazon review for **Snowflakes (Land of Fright™ #3 – in Collection I)**

Welcome to the Land of Fright™
A World of Spine Tingling Stories Filled with the Strange, the Eerie, and the Weird

# Land of Fright™

## Collection I

# JACK O'DONNELL

Visit www.landoffright.com

# DEDICATION

To all the writers who have ever thrilled me with their words. All those great books, all those great stories, all those wonderful imaginations gave me endless hours of bliss and escape. Thanks.

# LAND OF FRIGHT™
# COLLECTION I
# CONTENTS

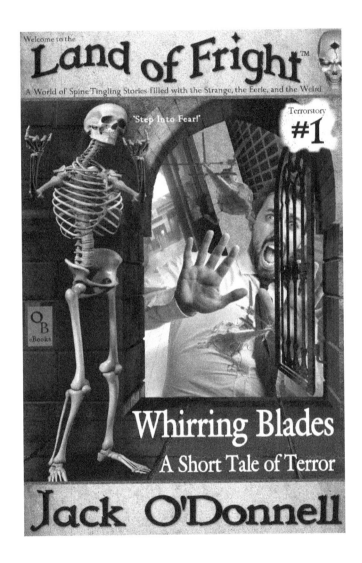

# TERRORSTORY #1
# WHIRRING BLADES

## Massacred Bodies Found at Local Mall

*GLENLAKE, IL (LFN) — Several brutally mutilated bodies were found by Hillview Mall office workers early Tuesday morning. A Glenlake detective said three victims were found at the scene, and what he believed to be the body parts of two more fatalities. Two of the victims have been identified as employees of the Gamer's Dreamland store located in the east wing of the mall.*

**"Y**ou ready to save the world, Lewis?"

Lewis Mclean looked up at his father to see him staring down at him. Lewis shrugged and smiled hesitantly. "Are you?" Lewis was twelve years old with wild, curly black hair. He was dressed in frayed jeans and a t-shirt that proclaimed '*I may be left handed, but I am always right.*'

His dad just grunted.

Lewis turned back to look at the large man standing near the front of the game store. The big black man looked nervous. Lewis thought that was strange. He didn't think he ever saw such a nervous security guard before. Maybe it was just because it was past the normal store hours and the rest of the mall was closed.

"Houston, I think we have a problem," Lewis heard someone mutter. He looked away from the security guard to the two young men working behind the counter. They both had very nervous faces all of a sudden. Lewis felt a quick rush of absolute despair. He knew what those looks meant.

"You're telling me we waited in this line for five hours for nothing?" Marty Mclean set his jaw. Marty was a burly man with a scrunched face and tight lips that made most people think he was ticked off all the time. But at this moment, Lewis knew his dad really was ticked off. The little twitch in the bottom of his dad's jaw always gave his anger away.

The clerk, whose Gamer's Dreamland name tag proclaimed as Jeff, looked nervously away from Marty. Jeff had unkempt brown hair and a narrow face pockmarked with acne scars. He clearly wanted nothing to do with this irate man scowling at him.

Another clerk, Tony, stepped up to the counter. "I'm sorry, sir." Tony had a thin mustache and a shadow of scruff on his face and neck; he absently scratched at his stubble.

"We had it reserved," Marty said.

Tony nodded. "I understand that. They didn't send us enough copies. This is the hottest game on the planet right now."

Lewis felt his insides shrivel. He looked up to see his father glancing down at him.

"Don't you fucking cry on me, Lewis."

Lewis knew he had the shimmering of tears in the corners of his eyes, but he quickly looked away so his father wouldn't see them.

"We were lucky to get as many copies as we did," Tony added.

Marty looked back over at Tony. "I'm not feeling very lucky."

Tony nervously stroked the stubble on his cheek. "I'm not either, believe me. You look like you can kick my ass with just your big toe." Tony glanced over at the security guard standing just inside the store near the demo kiosk.

Lewis followed Tony's gaze. The security guard was looking out into the mall corridor, paying no attention to what was happening in the store. Lewis looked back to his father. His dad's face remained even, his jaw tight. The twitch was there, a little more pronounced now.

"Let's just go, Dad," Lewis said. He pulled at his father's sleeve. He quickly wiped away the wetness that threatened at the corner of his eye.

"No, we're not going anywhere."

An odd humming sound filled the background. Lewis looked over to see the security guard shift his position and glance out deeper into the mall corridor. The game store was situated in a far corner of the single-story mall, on the eastern wing. To the left of the game store was a huge JT Barney's department store at the end of the wing, its entrance closed and gated hours ago. The security guard wasn't looking that way. He was looking right, towards the eastern corridor that was dotted with half a dozen other stores on either side of the hallway.

"We need to close the store, sir."

"After we get the game we waited six hours for, sure."

"I can't give you what I don't have," Tony told Marty.

The security guard finally moved. He eased over to them and cocked his head back towards the store entrance. He was a large black man with a round face and soft eyes. The name on his badge read Karamo Senghore. "You guys hear that?" the guard asked.

Tony looked at the guard, then at the door. "Hear what?"

"I don't know. I just hear something funny outside."

"Probably just the other idiots who waited seven hours for nothing," Marty said.

"Probably the cleaning people," Tony said.

"No, it's Monday. They don't work on Monday night," Karamo said.

"Technically it's Tuesday morning," Jeff said. He finished putting the store's deposit in the safe and pushed the heavy door shut. It closed with a metal clank.

"I want to speak to the manager," Marty said.

Tony looked away from the store's entrance to Marty. "I am the manager."

"What are we doing to do about this?" Marty asked.

"*We* need to lock up the store."

"So that's it? My son and I waited eight hours for nothing?"

"It's okay, Dad," Lewis said.

"No, it's not okay," Marty said, keeping his gaze on Tony.

"We'll get another shipment in next week. I can give you a call when it comes in."

Marty remained impassive. Twitch.

"I'm sorry. I can't give you what I don't have," Tony said again.

Lewis saw his dad just stare at Tony for a long moment. He could see the clenched tightness in his jaw.

"How the fuck do we get out of here?" Marty demanded.

Tony pointed. "The west entrance on the other side of the mall. Everything else is locked and gated up."

Marty grabbed Lewis by the hand and yanked his son towards the game store exit. "Let's go."

Lewis obediently followed his father out of the store, but suddenly stopped as they reached the large common area in the center of the mall.

Marty turned to look back at him, his face wrinkled with a foul attitude. "Come on."

"Dad, I think you should stop."

"What? Why?"

Lewis lifted his hand and pointed over his dad's shoulder.

"Is everybody seeing what I'm seeing?"

No one answered Tony. The five of them stood silently on the edge of the common area, taking in the scene before them.

A line of toy helicopters floated in the air in the middle of the common area. They hovered, bobbing slightly up and down. Their blades hummed and whistled and breathed as they whirled round and round. *Whupp whupp whupp.*

"Who the hell is controlling them?" Marty asked.

Lewis glanced around the area. He didn't see anyone else. There were several small closed-up kiosks dotting the large circular common area, booths that sold smartphones, massages, insurance, jewelry, and stuffed animals. Near those were numerous empty stone benches, a dozen fake plants, and a small fountain directly in the center, but no other people.

"It's Mandiki," Karamo said.

Marty looked at the security guard. "Mandiki? Who the hell is that?"

"My wife."

"Your wife?" Marty asked. "Your wife is controlling those?" He glanced around the common area. "Where is she?"

Karamo slowly raised his hand and pointed at the helicopters.

"Where? I don't see her," Jeff said.

"Okay, this is ridiculous. Tell her to knock it off." Marty took a step forward. "Where the hell is she?"

The helicopters reacted, several of them moving in Marty's path, forming an ominous wall of whirring blades. Their windshields looked like huge bulbous insect eyes. Marty grabbed Lewis's hand and held it tight, pulling his son protectively to his side.

"She is unhappy with me," Karamo said.

"This is stupid. I got things to do." Jeff bolted forward, making a move to go around the helicopters.

"Jeff, wait!" Tony shouted.

Jeff raced around a row of stone benches, skirting past some of the fake potted plants and the small fountain.

Several helicopters gave chase immediately. A bright blue helicopter dove low and its blades sliced through Jeff's skin, cutting the flesh in his calf. He was wearing cargo shorts, so his legs were exposed and an easy target for the whirring blades. Jeff howled and went down, clutching at his bleeding leg as blood spurted from the deep cut. Another helicopter, this one a bright lime green, swooped in and its blades made a clean cut right across Jeff's throat. Blood sprayed everywhere. A stream of red hit the helicopter's blades and the machine sputtered and dipped towards the ground. It faltered for a few more seconds, but then recovered, climbing back up into the air just as it was about to hit the ground.

The others were silent for a long moment. Everything had happened so fast they had no time to react.

Several dozen helicopters hovered above Jeff, holding a vigil over his death throes. He became still very quickly. The pool of blood around his body slowly enlarged.

"Holy shit... holy shit... holy shit..." Tony muttered the phrase over and over and over, unable to take his gaze away from Jeff's motionless body.

"What the fuck just happened?" Marty glared at Tony. "This some kind of stupid promotional stunt? You got cameras on us?" He raised a middle finger and swung it around in the air. "Here, you can use this."

Tony didn't answer. He just stared at the pool of blood growing larger and larger around Jeff's prone body. The helicopters buzzed around his corpse like flies on road kill.

"We need to get back in the store," Karamo said. His voice was amazingly calm.

No one moved. They couldn't look away from the gruesome growing rivers of red expanding around Jeff's body.

"We really need to get back in the store," Karamo said, his voice louder now, more insistent.

"We can't," Tony finally said, his gaze still locked on his dead co-worker.

"Why not?"

"Because Jeff has the keys."

Lewis looked back at Jeff's corpse. Several helicopters hovered above him, clearly keeping guard over his body.

Marty pointed at Jeff's prone body. "Are you telling me that is real?" He looked at Tony. "You really expect me to believe that? Come on, knock this shit off. I need to get my boy home." He looked back to Jeff's body. "Come on, kid, you can get up now!" he yelled at him.

"Mister, he is not getting up," Tony said.

Marty scowled at Tony, then looked at the big security guard. Karamo just stared back. "Is there another way out of here?" Marty asked. He pulled Lewis even tighter to his side.

Tony shook his head. "We have to get to the other side of the mall. All the other entrances are locked and gated. There's no way past them." He paused. "And we've got another three hours before anybody shows up."

"Shoot them," Lewis said.

The others looked at him.

"He's a security guard," Lewis said, motioning with his head to the large black man.

Tony and Marty looked expectantly at Karamo.

"Don't you have a gun?" Marty asked.

"Yes."

"Shoot the fucking things," Tony said.

"I don't have any bullets left," Karamo said.

"You don't have any bullets left?" Tony asked.

Marty frowned. "What the hell does that mean?"

"I used them."

"You used them? On what?"

Karamo did not answer.

Several of the helicopters rose up and away from Jeff's body. Then rotated in the air to face them. *Whupp whupp whupp.*

Lewis and Marty turned and raced towards the north corridor. Karamo followed them.

Tony skirted the other side of a long stone bench that split the corridor, separating himself from them on the opposite side of the wide pedestrian walkway.

Lewis, Marty, and Karamo reached a pop machine and ducked in behind it.

Sweat beaded on Lewis's forehead. His heart pounded hard in his chest, the sound filling his ears like waves crashing against a rocky shore. He chanced a quick glance around the pop dispensing machine and quickly pulled back as he saw six helicopters hovering at the entrance to the corridor. He struggled for a breath.

They had nowhere to go. The Coel's store at the far end of this corridor was also gated shut. Every other store in the corridor was barred by heavy metal grids.

Marty's breathing was more ragged now, too. Lewis could see that his dad was having a hard time catching his breath. "You okay, Dad?"

His dad dismissed his question with an impatient wave. He bent over, holding his hand to his side.

"Get over here with us," Karamo shouted at Tony.

"No, man. I'm good right here," Tony yelled back from across the corridor.

Lewis quickly fumbled in his pocket and pulled out his smartphone. He put it to his ear, but all he heard was *whupp whupp whupp*. He tried to dial different numbers, jabbed at different apps, but all he heard was the incessant sound of helicopter blades whirring. He slammed the phone back into his pocket.

The three of them stared at the hovering helicopters that waited at the entrance of the corridor.

"What the fuck are they waiting for?" Marty asked, his voice rising, nearly shrill.

"Me," Karamo said. "They are waiting for me. She's saving me for last."

"Who is?"

"My wife."

"Where the fuck is she?" Marty looked out into the corridor. "Where the fuck are you, you crazy bitch?" he shouted.

"She's right there."

They looked at Karamo to see him pointing at the helicopters.

"I don't see her," Marty said. "She hiding behind

something? Tell her to come the fuck out."

"She's not hiding. She's right there."

Lewis saw his dad's scowl deepen. He saw that his father couldn't stop his hands from trembling. His jaw twitched. "What the fuck is going on?" Marty demanded.

"She ran the Helicoptron kiosk," Karamo stated.

Lewis looked at Karamo, frowning deeply. "What?"

"She ran the Helicoptron kiosk," Karamo repeated.

"She sells those things?" Marty asked.

Karamo nodded. "She used to."

"Used to?"

Karamo nodded. "Yes." The big security guard looked at them. "Before I killed her."

Marty turned to stare at the big man. "You killed your wife?" he asked.

Karamo nodded. "Yes. And her lover." The big security guard looked at the helicopters then back to them. "I had to. They wanted to put a hex on me." Karamo shook his head and his large mass actually looked as if it shivered. "Bad black magic."

"You killed her and now she's inside those things?" Lewis asked.

Karamo nodded.

"How?" Lewis asked.

Karamo looked at him. "She's a bad woman. I thought bringing her here to this country would help her. I thought it would cleanse her. But it didn't. She just stayed ugly and mean. She has brought the poison of the old country here with her."

"Where did you come from?"

"Gambia."

Lewis stared mutely at Karamo. He had never heard of that country. "Where is that?"

"It is on the west coast of Africa. They still hunt and kill witches there. Like in your old Salem. That is why we had to leave."

"Because your wife was a witch?"

"Mandiki is a sorceress."

Marty shook his head. "That's just crazy talk. This is all just fucking crazy!"

The helicopters hovered at the end of the corridor. *Whupp whupp whupp.*

Lewis looked at Karamo. "For real?"

Karamo nodded. "She was very powerful in Gambia. The government was afraid of her. We escaped years ago and came here to start a new life." Karamo shook his head. "That is my mistake. I thought I could change her. I thought taking her out of Gambia would weaken her. But it didn't. I fear it only made her stronger." Karamo glanced down at the gun in his holster. "I tried to stop her. I tried. But she is too strong."

Lewis wracked his brain for all the ways you could kill a witch. There was the wicked witch from the Wizard of Oz. She got melted by a simple bucket of water. The witches in Salem got burned at the stake. He wasn't sure about any other witches. He never battled any witches in the games he played.

"Look, they're swarming!" Tony shouted from the other side of the corridor.

"Jesus," Marty exclaimed.

Lewis looked across the corridor at Tony, then looked back up the corridor, seeing more helicopters arriving to join the others that hovered at the entrance to the hallway. He looked at the cans in the pop machine Tony was huddled behind, then looked at the pop machine next to them. "Dad, give me two dollars."

"What?" Marty looked at Lewis with extreme annoyance. "Are you kidding me?"

"I have an idea." Lewis tapped on the side of the pop machine.

"No, knock it off. I need to think."

"Hurry, give me some money!"

Marty impatiently pulled a five out of his pocket and slapped it into Lewis's hand. "Shit, here."

Lewis grabbed it and moved to the front of the machine. He fed the bill into the machine. The machine spit it back. He quickly slid the bill over his pant leg, trying to smooth the wrinkled paper as best he could. He fed the smooth bill into the machine. The machine blipped and took the offering. Lewis jabbed at a button. The machine clicked and whined, then spit out a can of root beer. Quarters clanked down into the change slot. Lewis left them there.

The helicopters dipped their front ends, picking up speed, and raced down the corridor, heading straight for them.

"What the hell are you doing?" Marty demanded.

Lewis didn't answer. He grabbed the cold can and shook it furiously.

The helicopters quickly neared, the sounds of their whirring blades getting louder and louder. *WHUPP WHUPP WHUPP.*

"Lewis!" Marty shouted.

Lewis looked up just as one of the helicopters was almost on top of him. He snapped at the pull tab, jerking it back with a sharp tug. A brown blasting spray of carbonated sweet water erupted from the end of the can, showering the nearest helicopter with a sticky stream. The helicopter jerked back, tilting its head up as the spray struck it. Its blades sputtered and groaned. It suddenly jerked to the side, hitting the helicopter next to it, crashing into it with a loud crack. That sent the second helicopter swerving into the third. Their blades got tangled and snapped, sending black chunks of hard plastic scattering in several directions. The three helicopters plummeted to the ground in a heap. Their blades clicked and clacked as they struggled to be free of each other, but they were stuck fast together.

Karamo jumped out into the open and stomped on the helicopters, smashing them under his hard-soled black dress shoes. He then quickly moved back behind the pop machine.

Marty gripped Lewis around his forearm and yanked him back to his side. "Are you crazy!"

"Way to go!" Tony shouted from across the corridor.

Lewis looked across the corridor to Tony. The game store clerk was still hiding behind the pop machine on the other side of the pedestrian walkway.

"Watch out!" Lewis shouted.

Several helicopters were headed Tony's way now.

Tony fumbled in his pocket and pulled out a crumpled bill. He smoothed it on his leg just as Lewis had done, then fed the money into the machine. He quickly jabbed at a button and a can dropped into the slot. He snatched it and shook it, violently pumping the can up and down.

The helicopters raced towards him.

Tony pointed the can at them and flipped the pull tab.

But the liquid only dribbled out in a pale yellow stream.

The helicopters reached Tony and cut him up, tearing into the flesh in his arms, his chest, his face. Tony screamed and dropped the can, trying to protect himself as best he could. Red liquid sprayed out in all directions as Tony became the source of a fountain of blood.

Lewis watched the can roll towards them across the tiled floor. It was a can of lemonade. Non-carbonated.

"Jesus Christ," Marty muttered.

Lewis looked up to see his father's jaw flutter in discordant harmony with his trembling fingers.

The helicopters that killed Tony hovered about him, their blades buzzing and whirring.

More helicopters arrived at the edge of the corridor. They patiently hovered in the air. *Whupp whupp whupp.*

Weapons, Lewis thought. They needed some kind of weapons. He glanced at the nearby kiosks, trying to remember what each one of them contained. Then he saw a kiosk covered with a green tarp a few dozen feet down the corridor. He was pretty sure he knew what was underneath that tarp.

"Over here!" Lewis called out. He had waited until his dad was looking at the hovering helicopters before darting over to the kiosk. He grabbed the corner of the green tarp and lifted it up.

"Get back here!" Marty shouted to him, urging him with a sharp wave to get back behind the pop machine.

Lewis raised the tarp higher, revealing a row of foam pirate swords.

Karamo quickly moved over to Lewis, and Marty had no choice but to follow the big man.

"Take one," Lewis told them.

Karamo reached in under the tarp and squeezed the blade part of the fake weapon. Lewis knew it was firm, dense foam. He had two just like them at home. The security guard looked up at Lewis and nodded. Karamo grabbed a foam blade and handed it to Marty. "Take it."

Marty made no move to take the pirate sword.

"Damn it, man, take it!" Karamo demanded.

Marty took the foam sword.

Karamo reached in and grabbed two for himself and had to react immediately as two helicopters swooped in towards him. *Whupp whupp whupp.* He swung the foam blade in his right hand, shielding his face, and hit the helicopter square in its small frame. The blow sent the helicopter careening towards the gumball kiosk stand nearby. It hit one of the containers, shattering the glass. Gumballs spilled everywhere, a rainbow of colored orbs scattering in every direction across the tiled floor.

Lewis took out one helicopter with a fierce slashing strike, bringing the sturdy foam blade straight down on top of the whirring blades. The helicopter dropped like a rock. "Take that, fucker!"

Marty went for a strike, but stepped on some gumballs and lost his footing. He went down, his arms flailing, as a red helicopter dove towards his head. The whirring blades snipped off a few locks of his hair, narrowly missing taking out a piece of his forehead.

But the second red helicopter didn't miss.

Its slashing blades gouged a chunk of flesh out of Marty's right cheek, then tilted up to slice through his eye. Marty shrieked in pain and terror, clutching at his face. Blood spilled through his fingers.

"Dad!" Lewis quickly moved over to him, swinging strongly, taking the helicopters down with two quick slashing strikes. The helicopters hit the ground near him and Lewis quickly stomped on them, hearing very satisfactory crunches beneath his gym shoes. He quickly dropped to his knees at his father's side. Blood from his dad's spurting cuts splashed into Lewis's face, onto his chest.

Marty clutched futilely at his face, shrieking, unable to staunch the rain of blood erupting from the gashes in his face and eye.

Lewis clumsily put his hands over his father's fingers, trying to stop the flowing blood.

Karamo moved to their side, nudging Lewis back. He ripped off a piece of Marty's shirt with a savage yank and crumbled the piece into a ball. He pushed Marty's hands out of the way and held the cloth tightly against the wounds. He grabbed Marty's hand and put it on top of the cloth, pushing firmly against the cut. "Hold it here. Press it tight. You'll be okay."

"Okay, okay," Marty managed to mumble. He slowed his breathing, fumbling at the cloth as best he could. "Jesus." A lone tear slipped out of his good eye.

"Don't you fucking cry on me, Dad. You know how much I hate tears," Lewis said softly. He felt his own tears pouring out of his eyes and he just let them come. They mingled with the splashes of blood that had hit him from his father's spurting cuts. They were just supposed to pick up a video game and go home. That's it. A simple trip to the mall. A simple trip. He was supposed to be at home sitting on his couch killing monsters.

*Whupp whupp whupp.*

Lewis looked up to see more helicopters hovering nearby. There were still at least two dozen helicopters remaining. They bobbed up and down slightly, forming a living wall of deadly blades.

But then they did something unexpected.

They slowly descended to the ground, each helicopter easing down to the mall floor, their blades slowing, then finally stopping. The *whupp whupp whupp* of their whirring blades faded away into silence.

And then it was quiet.

They stared at the parked helicopters for a long moment.

"Jesus, are they done?" Marty muttered. Blood still slowly seeped out from beneath the cloth he held tightly to his wound.

A very loud rumble sounded behind them. Karamo and Lewis rose up away from Marty and slowly turned around. Marty craned his neck, turning toward the source of the loud noise.

And they all just stared for a long moment.

A remote control toy tank slowly rolled forward, its olive-green hull dotted with camouflage stripes. Behind the lead tank, more tanks inched forward. The remote control tank kiosk was visible just behind the vehicles.

The lead tank moved closer. Its muzzle stared

them down, a black cyclopean eye promising death from its darkness.

"I'm sorry," Karamo said.

Lewis turned to look at Karamo with questioning eyes. He saw the look change on Karamo's face. He had looked nervous before, but now he could see the big man's face filling with absolute terror.

"He was the one cheating with my wife," Karamo said.

The tanks rumbled closer.

*You ready to save the world, Lewis?* His dad's question rang through Lewis's mind again. Lewis knew the answer. He wasn't ready. He wasn't ready at all.

The muzzle flash of a dozen cannons was the last thing they ever saw.

*GLENLAKE , Il (LFN) updated 7:52 AM CST — According to Glenlake authorities, several dozen remote control helicopters and remote control tanks are still missing. Residents are urged to contact local police if they have any information that might help solve this robbery and find the perpetrators of these horrific murders.*

# TERRORSTORY #2
# THE BIG LEAGUES

## Just one hit. That's all he wanted.

"You okay, Samuel?" his father asked.

Samuel nodded. He was a lanky kid with a crooked nose, awkward knobby knees, and fumbling long arms. He was not graceful in his movements, not by a long shot. He re-gripped the baseball bat, holding it tight in his long fingers.

"Just watch the ball."

Samuel nodded. He readied himself at the plate. He tapped the tip of the bat down on home plate like he'd seen the big ball players do on TV. Some of them grabbed their crotches, but he thought that was too vulgar so he skipped that part. And the spitting.

That was just nasty, too. He didn't like all the spitting.

"Here it comes."

He waited as his father wound up and hurled the ball in his direction. Eager and anxious to hit the ball, he swung. Way too early. He was done swinging before the ball even reached him. The ball sailed past him, bounced on the ground and hit the metal chain link fence that formed a quarter circle behind home plate. The clinking metallic sound was a sound he had heard far too often. He hadn't hit a ball yet. Not even a foul tip.

"Too early," his father said. "That's okay." He bent down and picked out another ball from the bucket of balls situated near the pitcher's mound next to the rubber. "Get in your stance. Turn more sideways. Okay, good."

This time Samuel was determined not to swing early. He watched the ball release from his father's hand and he waited. And then he swung. Way too late. The ball was already bouncing on the ground behind him when he swung. It clanked against the metal fence.

Just one hit. Just to hear the bat crack against that white rawhide one time. One hit in one real game. That's all he wanted.

<hr />

"This is how you'll help the team win. I'm coaching this team to be the champs, not the chumps."

"But I want to hit the ball."

"Kid, you can't hit. We both know that, right?" Coach Aaron said. "That kid on the mound has got the fastest pitch in the league. You don't stand a chance. If it was up to me, you wouldn't even be playing. But it ain't up to me. Rules say I gotta let you bat at least once and play an inning. Just let him hit you. We need you to get on base. It won't hurt for long, kid. I swear."

"My name is Samuel."

"Whatever. You're up."

Samuel moved to the batter's box and took his stance, setting his feet square to the plate. He tapped the end of the bat on home plate and gripped the bat tight. The first pitch came in before he was even ready for it.

"Steeerike," the umpire yelled, thrusting his finger out to the side.

Loud groans filled the air all around him.

Samuel felt some sweat beading on his forehead. He did his best to ignore it. He readied himself for the second pitch.

The pitcher wound up and Samuel swung.

Then the ball hit the catcher's mitt with a resounding slap against the worn leather. "Steeerike," the umpire called out, thrusting two fingers out to the side.

Laughter filtered in from the bleachers behind the home plate backstop fence.

Samuel glanced over to see a venomous glare on Coach's crinkly face. Coach Aaron had a deep tan on his broad features, and the permanent scowl on his features made his skin look like old crinkled-up paper. Coach Crinkly Face, he called him, but just to himself. He wouldn't dare to say that out loud to anybody.

Samuel looked at the runners on first, second, and third. The bases were loaded. It was the bottom of the ninth. They were down by one run. And here he was at the plate. It was a baseball player's dream come true.

But for Samuel it was just a nightmare. He readied himself for the next pitch. He had a feeling it was going to be a fastball. The pitcher had him up 0-2. He had several pitches to waste.

The pitcher wound up and fired the ball towards home plate.

Samuel knew he couldn't let his team down. Not now. Not in the last game of the season. Not when the championship was on the line. He did what he knew he had to do. He leaned far over the plate and looked up to see a huge white orb heading straight for his face.

The victory was sweet. The kids laughed and cheered. The parents whooped and applauded. Backs were slapped. Hands were shook. Trophies were hoisted high. It was a good day to be ten years old and playing for the Woodglen Warriors.

An ambulance pulled away from the park, its siren not even loud enough to drown out the sounds of jubilant celebration coming from the field.

The hospital room for Samuel was a very understated affair. A single balloon floated near the small window. His father visited often and sat quietly by his bedside. Several times tears fell from his father's eyes, and he would sometimes just let them slide down his cheek, or sometimes he would wipe them away with the backs of his fingers. A priest stopped by. "Just in case Samuel didn't wake up," Father McCafferty said. A teacher from his school sent a card. None of his teammates or their parents or Coach Aaron came to see him.

It came in the mail in a shiny white envelope. Coach Aaron Goldfarb looked at the logo in the upper left corner again. Very stylish, he thought. The vertical line of each 'T' was in the shape of a baseball bat and each 'O' was in the shape of a baseball. He read the words again. *Traveling Team Tournament of Champions.* He grabbed his gold-plated letter opener and sliced open the envelope flap. His fingers trembled with excitement as he pulled out the folded piece of paper and opened it.

It was an invitation. An invitation to compete in the Traveling Team Tournament of Champions. The Woodglen Warriors were finally going to be on the big stage. A single elimination event. You win, you keep playing. You lose, you're done.

Aaron smiled. Time for the big leagues. All of his hard work was finally paying off. All the time and effort. All the sacrifices. Finally, these stupid a-holes recognized his brilliance as a coach. He reached into his pocket for his phone. Time to tell everyone to clear their calendars.

"You sure this it?" a father asked. The man squinted behind his small oval glasses. Aaron could never remember the guy's name. He just knew he was the second baseman's dad.

Aaron nodded. "That's what the invitation said."

"Looks like a forest preserve. I don't see a baseball field."

The dozen cars that made up the transportation crew for the Woodglen Warriors were parked neatly in a row in the marked off parking spaces. Near the asphalt parking lot was an open picnic area. A bit farther beyond that was a covered gazebo, its wood walls in desperate need of a new coat of paint. Half a dozen rusted charcoal grills dotted the area.

"There's a path," Karl shouted. He was a short and stout kid with a freckled face, perfectly suited for his position on the team. He pointed to a trail leading through the trees at the east end of the parking lot. It was like a tunnel, with the trees curving over and touching each other fifty feet up in the air to form a corridor lined with tree bark and leaves. He whooped and raced toward the path, clutching his catcher's mask tightly in his hand.

"Hey, get back here!" Aaron shouted at him. Karl shuffled back to him. Aaron pointed to a bag of bats. "Grab some equipment. Coach leads the way."

Aaron stepped into the open area at the end of the path and paused. He smiled. The playing field was well maintained with low cut grass and a smoothly raked infield. The dugouts were above-ground benches enclosed by chain-link fences on the sides and top, giving them the appearance of long, narrow cages. A narrow doorway led into each dugout.

Aaron mentally gauged the distance to the right

field fence from home plate. About 200 feet. Karl could probably clock one over the fence. He smiled. Especially if he gave him some *juice* in his juice. A large screen filled the right field area just past the outfield fence. A huge scoreboard filled up the left side of the area beyond the outfield fence.

Just beyond the scoreboard and the big screen were dense woods. The baseball field was surrounded on all sides by thick trees. From what he could see, the path they had just walked up was the only way in and out of the field. This is different, Aaron thought. But he had to admit it was a pretty cool looking baseball field.

The other team was already there. There were nine players on the field, each standing in their respective positions. They were all tall and kind of lanky. The pitcher stood on the mound. The catcher stood behind the plate. Aaron looked at them for a moment and frowned. None of them were moving. They stood as still as statues. He looked at the first baseman, who was the player closest to him, but he wasn't moving either. He tried to make out their faces but for some reason he couldn't bring them into focus. He looked at the second baseman and the shortstop, but their faces refused to come into view. They reminded him of standees in a movie theater. Aaron blinked several times. His frown deepened. They still hadn't moved.

Aaron turned when he heard footsteps step up behind him, seeing Karl stepping up next to him. "Hey Karl, do you see that?"

"See what?" Karl asked as he reached him.

Aaron turned back to the field and pointed at the players. "That." But now the players were moving.

The pitcher threw a pitch right down the middle and the catcher caught it, then tossed it back. The first basemen threw a grounder to the second baseman, doing typical warm up throws. The second basemen scooped it up and fired the ball back to the first baseman.

"Wow, cool field!" Frankie said. He was a tall kid with dark Italian features and jet black hair. He kept going and raced on by.

Aaron stared at the opposing team on the field for a long moment. He glanced over at the home team dugout. There were about seven or eight figures sitting on the wooden bench. None of them moved. There was a spectator stands on either side of the field. The home team stands were filled. But none of the people in the stands were moving either. He looked closer at them. They were only wearing two sets of clothes amongst them. All the men were in identical blue jeans and white t-shirts and the women in identical pink dresses. Great, he mentally moaned. Fan uniforms. These guys are serious.

The rest of his team and the parents walked past him, talking amongst themselves, marveling at the baseball field hidden inside a forest preserve. They didn't seem to notice anything out of the ordinary. He followed them towards the visiting team dugout.

The parents made their way to the stands, finding seats. "Let's slaughter these clowns, Coach," one of the parents said as she walked past him.

Aaron walked through the narrow dugout entrance. His boys all sat on the bench, waiting for his instructions. "You guys ready to kill these bozos?"

Heads nodded in firm affirmation. "Fuck yeah," a voice said. Some of the boys giggled at that.

Suddenly, a squawk and a crackling sound filled the air. Aaron turned towards the right field fence and the big screen beyond it. Images flickered across its surface. Coach Aaron immediately recognized himself up on the screen.

*"Put your cleats up when you slide,"* Coach Aaron said. *"Some of them don't have shin guards on. That's their problem, not ours."*

*Frankie nodded.*

*"That'll slow 'em down. Maybe they miss the next grounder because they got a little hobble in their step. It's the little things that make a difference if we're gonna win."* Aaron looked at Frankie. *"You do want to win, don't you?"*

*"Heck, yeah,"* Frankie said.

What the hell is this? Aaron wondered. He looked at Frankie. "You seeing this?"

Frankie nodded.

The screen flickered and another scene played out.

*"Talk about his mother,"* Coach Aaron said to Karl. *"Just whisper it, but make sure he hears it. She's a slut. Let him know that you know. You gotta rattle him. Get inside his head and mess with it."*

*Karl gripped his catcher's mask and nodded.*

*"Let him settle in to his position. Let him get comfortable in the box. Then tell him you know all his mother's dirty secrets."*

*Karl laughed.*

"Hey, that's me," Karl said.

Aaron glanced down to see Karl standing next to him.

"Why are they showing videos of us?" Karl asked.

"I don't know," Aaron answered absently. The muscles in his face tightened. "But I intend to find out." He glanced around the field, looking for the other team's coach, or any official he could find. He spotted the head umpire heading over in his direction. He moved towards him. "Hey," he called out to the umpire. He pointed up to the screen. "What the hell is that? Where did you get those videos?"

"Are you ready?" the umpire asked. He had his mask on already and it was difficult to make out his face.

Aaron frowned. "No, I'm not ready." He pointed at the screen again with a jabbing finger. "What the hell is that?"

"Are you ready?" the umpire calmly repeated.

"No, I'm not ready. Where's the other coach?"

The umpire pointed to the large screen.

Aaron looked up at the screen. Now the screen displayed the inside of a hospital room. A young boy lay motionless on the bed. Numerous machines were hooked up to him, monitors blipping and flashing and beeping with steady, monotonous rhythms. Suddenly, a face filled the screen, startling Aaron. "Hi, guys," a young boy said. He waved a quick, spastic wave of his hand as his face filled the screen.

"What the hell?" Aaron muttered.

"It's that kid," Karl said.

Aaron looked down to see Karl again standing next to him. "What?"

"That kid, you know."

"What kid?"

"That kid who took the fastball in his face."

Aaron frowned. Another scene lit up the video screen and his frown deepened.

> *"I'm not into this pansy everybody's a winner bullshit. We win because we score more runs than the other team, not because you put on a clean uniform and show up for the game. Just stick your face over the plate. It won't hurt for long."*
>
> *"I don't want to get hit."*
>
> *"You want to help the team win, don't you?"*
>
> *"Yes."*
>
> *"This is how you'll help the team win because you can't bat for shit. I'm coaching this team to be the champs, not the chumps."*
>
> *"But I want to hit the ball."*
>
> *"Kid, you can't hit. We both know that, right? You haven't hit a ball all year. You suck. You think you're gonna hit a ball now? T-ball's more your speed. Though I bet you'd probably fucking miss that, too. That kid's got the fastest pitch in the league. You don't stand a chance because you suck more than a baby finding its fucking thumb for the first time. If it was up to me, you wouldn't even be playing. But it ain't up to me. Rules say I gotta let you bat at least once and play an inning. If you don't bat, we forfeit, kid. I ain't about to fucking forfeit a game."*
>
> *"My name is Samuel."*
>
> *"Whatever."*

Aaron looked over at the opposing team's bench. They all sat quietly, stiffly on the bench. They all stared at the field. Then, one of the boys slowly turned his head and looked at Aaron. He felt his heart seize in his chest.

The boy had no face.

Aaron looked for the tunnel path, but it was gone. He spun, looking, searching, but there was no path. They were encircled by giant trees. "Where is the path?"

"Victory opens the path to glory," the umpire said.

"What?"

"If you win, you can leave. You do want to win, don't you?"

"Let's go, we're leaving now!" Aaron declared.

"I would not suggest that." The umpire pointed to the nearby stands. All of the parents were now manacled to the steel stands, their mouths muffled with tape. "If you forfeit, you all die. We'll save your wife for the seventh inning stretch. I hope she's flexible."

Aaron looked at the umpire. "What the hell do you want?"

"Play ball!" Samuel shrieked from the large screen.

"Batter up," the umpire called.

"No!"

"Frankie, get up there."

Frankie stomped his foot down. "No!"

Aaron looked over at the parents, at his wife. Kelly's eyes were wide, completely filled with fear. Thick tape was plastered across her lips, keeping her silent. He looked at the dead body of Josh's mother in the center of the stands. He had refused to start the game and the chains had just tightened around her wrists, the manacles smashing through flesh, crunching through bone. The blood just kept spurting and spurting. Most of the bound parents in the stands were now covered in her blood. Aaron looked down at the line in the grass, a white chalk line separating the dugout area from the stands. "Anybody crosses that," the umpire had told him. "The bleacher bums blow up."

Aaron looked back to Frankie. "Frankie, get your ass up there and hit the damned ball."

"No!"

Aaron grabbed a bat and shook it in Frankie's face, his upper lip curling into a snarl. "Frankie, so help me, get up there and bat or I'll bash your head in."

Frankie glared at him and ripped the bat out of Aaron's hand. "You did this to us!"

Aaron said nothing. He watched Frankie approach the plate with hesitant steps.

The faceless pitcher on the mound followed Frankie's every step, slowly swiveling his head to keep his eyeless bead straight on Frankie.

Frankie settled into the batter's box. Aaron watched him re-grip the bat several times as he waited for the pitch.

The pitcher wound up and threw.

Thwack. To his surprise, Frankie hit a solid ball right up the middle. But he stood motionless at the plate, still clutching the bat.

"Jesus, run," Aaron muttered. "Run!" he shouted.

Frankie tossed the bat and darted off to first, making it safely to the bag. He smiled and waved at the bench.

Aaron turned to the bench with a nervous smile. "See. You guys can do this."

"I know what you did," the faceless catcher said.

Karl looked back at the catcher. He couldn't see any face behind the grill of the mask, couldn't see any mouth, but he was certain the catcher had spoken the words.

"I know what you did to that cat. It wasn't an accident."

Karl nervously looked away from the catcher, re-gripping the bat.

The pitcher threw a pitch and Karl let it go by.

"Steee-riike!" The umpire shouted it like it was two distinct words.

"I know what kind of sounds it made," the catcher said. "You still hear the sounds in your head, don't you? Sometimes when you are laying in bed at night, you hear the sounds, don't you?"

Karl said nothing as the catcher threw the ball back to the pitcher.

"You think it's in the same room with you sometimes, don't you?"

Karl did not respond. He could feel sweat beading up on his forehead, but he didn't wipe it away with his wristband like he usually did; he just left the wet sheen right where it was on his skin.

"Strike!" The umpire made a broad two-finger gesture.

The catcher rose up and threw the ball back to the pitcher. "Strike two," he said. He crouched back down and punched the palm of his mitt. "One more and you are out." The faceless catcher paused. "For good."

The faceless pitcher readied himself for the next pitch.

The catcher made a signal to the pitcher, the edge of his finger sliding across his throat.

Karl shifted in the batter's box. He licked his lips and re-gripped the bat.

The pitcher wound up and threw. The ball raced towards Karl.

A horrible caterwauling sound erupted from the catcher, startling Karl. He swung wildly at the pitch, missing the ball by a wide margin. Karl looked around with huge wide eyes. His feet were frozen in the batter's box. He couldn't feel his legs. He couldn't get them to move, no matter how much how he wanted to run.

Suddenly, the umpire stepped forward and slashed Karl's throat with a straight razor that suddenly appeared in his hand. Karl gurgled once and then collapsed.

"Yer out!" the umpire shrieked.

Aaron startled violently, leaping back away from the horrible scene he just witnessed. "Oh my God…"

All the kids in the dugout started screaming and yelling and shouting and screaming even more. One of the boys wet himself. Josh just sat on the bench, rocking back and forth, blubbering to himself about his mother.

Two men in clean white uniforms suddenly appeared and pulled Karl's body away, dragging it off the field. Or at least they had the rough semblance of men. They had faces, but their eyes were just black pinpoints, their noses more like tiny bumps and their mouths were just red slits. They made the beginnings of a pile behind the home plate fence with Karl's body.

The umpire wiped the blood from the plate with his umpire's brush. "Batter up!" he called out.

Nicky stood in the on-deck circle, unable to move. He looked down at his feet, puzzled that they wouldn't work. He was a lean kid with long brown hair. All the girls loved his cute dimples when he smiled. He wasn't smiling now.

"Nicky, get up there," Aaron called to him.

Nicky did not move.

"Nicky! Get up there and just hit the ball."

Finally, Nicky moved to the plate. He stared down at the red-stained sand beneath his feet, then readied himself for the pitch. After missing the first pitch, he managed to hit a ground ball to shortstop. The shortstop scooped it up and tossed it to the second baseman who had darted over to the second base bag. The second baseman caught the ball, tagged second base, then threw the ball to first. The first baseman caught the ball, his foot firmly planted on the first base bag.

The pile of bodies behind the home plate fence grew by two.

The ground ball sped towards Carlos.

It was the bottom of the first inning and the Woodglen Warriors were on the field now. Carlos was the back-up second baseman, taking Nicky's place. He was a quick little Hispanic kid with fast feet and fast hands. He wasn't a better hitter than Nicky was, but he was good on the field.

Sweat dripped down Carlos's face, stinging his eyes. But he kept his focus on the ball. It hit the edge of the dirt just past the grassy pitcher's mound and took a weird hop. Carlos raised his mitt and caught the ball. He quickly dug it out of his mitt and hurled it at Chuck, the first baseman.

Chuck kept his left foot on the edge of the first base bag and stretched for the ball, reaching the mitt on his right hand out as far as he could. The ball slapped against the palm of his mitt. The base jostled a second later as the runner hit the bag.

"Out!" the umpire yelled.

Chuck turned to see the runner stop dead in his tracks. The faceless player stood motionless for a long moment, still facing in the direction he had been running. Then, his form started to cave in, his body disintegrating, crumbling to dust. And then he was gone, the dust of his body scattered in the wind.

Chuck turned back towards the pitcher's mound. He and the pitcher, a lean and lanky kid named Billy, just stared at each other. Finally, Billy motioned for him to throw him the ball. Chuck frowned at him. Billy pointed to Chuck's mitt. Chuck looked down at his mitt, then remembered that he still held the ball. He threw it back to Billy.

The next faceless boy hit a double. A clean shot to right center.

The next faceless boy hit a solid grounder. The ground ball sped towards Carlos. Sweat dripped down his face, stinging his eyes, but he kept his focus on the ball. Until it went right through his legs.

The faceless boy who was on second base scored, racing across home plate. His faceless teammates were eerily silent. The faceless fans jumped up and down and waved their hands widely, but no sounds came out of their blank faces. It was an oddly eerie sight.

The two man-things in white uniforms moved over to the stands, unshackling a woman from the metal bench.

"What are they doing?" Aaron asked.

"Keeping score," the umpire answered.

Aaron startled at the umpire's voice. The umpire hadn't been anywhere near him just a second ago, but now he was standing right next to him. Aaron watched with growing dread as the men in white steered the woman towards a set of stairs that led up to the scoreboard platform. The woman stomped and squirmed, but it was no use; the men held onto her firmly and there was no escaping their grasp. The platform held two rows of hooks, a row of hooks just to the left of the center post and another row of hooks to the right, one row for each team. They led the woman to the row of hooks to the right, the row representing the home team. They lifted her up abruptly and slammed her down on one of the hooks, sinking the hook into her upper back. The woman flailed, kicking her legs wildly, throwing her arms up and down in spasmodic motions.

The men in white ripped the thick tape off her lips so everyone could hear her scream. Somehow the clothes of the two men stayed immaculately white no matter what they did or how near they were to the spraying blood; none of the spurting torrents of red liquid touched them.

"My God…" was all Aaron could mutter.

"Yes, it's a bit distracting. But don't worry. They usually stop squirming after a minute or two," the umpire said. "See, she's stopped already."

Aaron's face could not turn any whiter.

"Batter up!"

Carlos sat in the dirt at the edge of the infield in front of his second baseman position, crying.

Aaron walked up to Carlos. "Carlos, get up."

Carlos did not move.

"Carlos, you have to get up." Aaron reached for his arm and pulled him to his feet.

Carlos yanked his arm away, stepping away from the coach. "You did this. You did this to us." His stare was full of venom and hate.

Aaron grabbed his arm again, squeezing him tightly. He yanked Carlos towards him. "You watch your mouth, kid. You weren't complaining when we won all those games, were you? You weren't complaining about all those trophies you got, did you?" He squeezed his arm tighter. "Keep playing or they'll kill you." He shoved Carlos towards his position.

Carlos tripped and fell. Tears streamed down his face. He staggered to his feet and made his way towards his position. And then he kept on walking, heading towards the outfield.

Everyone just watched him in stunned silence.

Carlos reached the edge of the outfield fence and stopped, staring at the massive wall of thick trees just beyond. He tossed his mitt down and climbed over the fence. He stood on the other side of the fence, again just staring at the dark trees before him. Then the ground erupted around Carlos and skeletal hands pulled at him, clawing at him, dragging him beneath the earth. He didn't even scream. After a moment, he was gone, as if he never existed at all.

"Would you like to put in another player, coach?" the umpire asked. "We allow unlimited substitutions in our tournament."

"What happened to Carlos?" Aaron asked, staring numbly at the torn up patch of grass where Carlos had just been standing.

"Oh, he died," the umpire said. "He's not much use to you anymore, anyway, is he? Especially if he can't help you win."

The other boys on the bench looked on in terror. Josh sat on the bench, his face filthy with tears and dirt.

"Are you going to adjust your line up, coach?" the umpire asked.

Aaron continued to stare at the empty ground for a moment, then forced himself to look away into the dugout. He pointed to Josh. "Josh, shortstop."

Josh sat frozen on the bench.

"Josh, get out there."

Josh did not move.

Aaron leaned in close to him. "Josh, they'll kill your parents if you don't get out there."

"His parents are already dead," someone said.

A quick flash of the four bodies hanging on the scoreboard hooks burst into Aaron's head. Jesus, the kid's parents were hanging on two of those hooks. He forced the image away and turned to another boy.

"Timmy, get out there."

Timmy clutched at his mitt, his bloodshot eyes filled with terror. Then, he rose and moved out onto the field.

And so the madness of the game continued. Billy the pitcher was picked off during a rundown, killed between second and third base; the faceless third baseman knocked him down when he tagged him and then several other faceless boys stomped him to death right there on the field. Timmy struck out and joined the bodies behind the home plate fence. More outs. More deaths. More scores by the team of faceless boys. More bodies of parents hung on hooks. More spurting, splashing, spraying rivers of blood.

"Make it stop!" Aaron screamed. "Make it stop!"

A faceless figure gripping a bat came up to Aaron.

Aaron looked blankly at the boy.

A face started to take shape. Eyes appeared. A crooked nose appeared.

Aaron just watched.

The boy extended his arm and a finger pointed to home plate.

Aaron hesitated.

The finger became more insistent, jabbing towards home plate.

Aaron moved towards the plate, stepping onto the

blood-stained, five-sided slab of white rubber.

The boy moved to the batter's box, taking position, moving into a perfect batting stance. The boy gripped the bat tightly in his hands. He paused to tug at his crotch, then re-gripped the bat.

The umpire pushed Aaron's shoulders down, pushing him down to his knees over home plate.

"What do you want, kid?" Aaron asked.

A mouth appeared. The boy turned his head and spat out a blob of thick spit. He turned back to look at Coach Aaron. "My name is Samuel, Coach Crinkly Face. My name is Samuel."

Thwack! The hit was solid. Very solid.

# TERRORSTORY #3
# SNOWFLAKES

## Leeanla smiled a bright radiant smile.

This was not just any snowfall, she knew. It was The Snow. It fell from the sky in a sparkling, scintillating swirl of shimmering white flakes. It was the only snow that mattered in their entire life. The cold wind whirled around her, but she barely felt it. Her thick parka kept her warm.

She pushed her hood down away from her face and gazed up into the falling white snow, scanning, searching, probing the dense drizzle of frozen water. But this wasn't normal water. This was a gift from the gods. Once every ten years it fell from the sky. And she was old enough now to know what it meant. She brushed a lock of her brown hair away from her hazel eyes and continued to stare up into the falling snow.

Would she find hers? She had just turned eighteen, so it could happen. After all, it had happened in the past to others who had just reached adulthood. More than once. It actually had happened more often than should have been possible. Her hopes were very high. She had been good to the gods, offering them prayer and love like a devoted faithful student. No one else went to the shrine on Alabaster Hill as much as she did. No one else spoke their prayers with as much passion as she did during Communal. She hoped the gods were good to her in return. She was certain she was worthy. She was probably more worthy than any of the others in the group.

Katya was a nice girl, but she was kind of stupid. She couldn't do the simplest math equations in her head. She always had to write things down to figure them out. Leeanla couldn't conceive of a reason why the gods would choose Katya to be a ruler of men. Unless they had a cruel sense of humor.

Arkran was smart, but he was a real hot head. He always gave in to his emotional surges and had fits of both extreme rage and wild giddiness. He wasn't the most stable in the group. She had a sense that he would lead the men into more wars than he would prevent.

Leeanla gazed up into the mass of falling white flakes that covered the sky. So many snowflakes. All of them different. All of them filled with the possibility of bestowing the Miracle upon a chosen few. But only one of them was meant for her. Would she find it? Would she find hers first?

She saw a snowflake glint as it drifted down

towards her. Was that hers? By the gods, was that hers? She reached up and caught it in her open palm, then pulled her hand back down to study the flake. The flakes never melted right away if they were a gift from the gods. Normal snowflakes would only sit in her palm for a few seconds before they dissolved into a wet smear. She stared at the flake but immediately knew it wasn't hers; the snowflake faded into a clear splotch of water.

Then she heard a triumphant yelp of absolute glee. She felt an instant rush of excitement throughout her entire body. She knew what that sound meant. She looked over to see Arkran staring at his palm. He danced excitedly, nervously, unable to contain himself.

Leeanla moved quickly over to Arkran. "Are you sure?" she asked him.

Arkran looked up at her and Leeanla knew the answer. His blue eyes were brighter than she had ever seen them. He knew. She glanced down at what he held in his hand. The snowflake glittered in his palm. It was not dissolving. It was not fading away. Leeanla looked back up to his face. The snowflake in his palm clearly matched the snowflake marking on his left cheek. It was a perfect match. It was his. It belonged to Arkran. She looked back at the snowflake in his palm, then glanced back up into the sky. Where was hers? It wasn't fair. Why was Arkran first? She should have been first.

"Are you going to eat it?" someone asked.

In response, Arkran popped the snowflake into his mouth.

Everyone watched in absorbed silence.

"What does it taste like?"

Arkran was quiet for a long moment. He closed his eyes. And then dropped to his knees in the thick snow. His arms fell limply to his sides. He raised his face skyward. The snowflake mark on his cheek brightened, the center of it glowing first, then the light radiated outward to each of the six dendrites, filling every delicate line in the snowflake's arms with light.

They gathered around him, watching, waiting.

Snowflakes gently dropped onto Arkran's skin, glowing for a brief moment before being absorbed into his body. And then his eyes sprang open. They twinkled and sparkled with dazzling points of light. "It tastes like Heaven," Arkran said.

"How… how do you feel?" someone asked.

Arkran slowly rose to his feet. He steadily looked at the others standing around him, his gaze unhurriedly moving from face to face. "I feel—*right.*" He reached Leeanla with his gaze and she beamed him a bright smile. She waited for him to stop looking at the others and smile at her, but his gaze just kept moving steadily to the others near her.

The others around him smiled. Some nodded. Leeanla frowned. Arkran already seemed different within seconds of starting his transformation. More distant. More aloof. She wondered what kind of fantastic bits of insight were racing through his mind right now. Snowflakes gently dropped onto his skin, glowing for a brief moment before being absorbed into his body. Thousands of years of history and wisdom and knowledge were filling his brain.

And most importantly the secret to eternal youth. The gods included that little extra bonus of immortality to give the men they were to rule continuity in their leaders. Leeanla so wanted to live forever. The men she would rule could admire her beauty for generation after generation. They would bow to her wisdom and seek out her guidance in all important matters. She would rule them well. Strongly, but with kind firmness.

Leeanla wanted to reach out and touch Arkran's hand but she hesitated. She didn't want to disturb his moment of transformation. She was so happy for him! Arkran was a good friend. She fought back the pang of jealousy that stabbed at the thought of her friend's joy.

She looked back up at the sky, resuming her search. She muttered a soft prayer, mindful not to let a begging tone creep into her silent words.

"Katya found hers!"

Leeanla pulled her gaze from the swirling whiteness and looked over to the group huddled around Katya. Katya wasted no time in popping the snowflake into her mouth. She didn't drop to her knees like Arkran had done. She threw her hands out wide, turning her face up to the heavens. The flakes seemed to slow as they neared her skin, gently alighting on her face. Her snowflake on her cheek started to glow, the soft light starting at the heart of the flake, then moving out to the spindly arms just as Arkran's had done.

Leeanla glanced over at Arkran. The snowflake marking on his cheek was nearly fully lit; the very tips of the snowflake's arms glowed just a touch brighter than the rest of the flake. The knowledge of the Ancients was quickly filling him now. He knew their history, knew their strengths, their weaknesses. He would be able to intervene in the skirmishes of men and give them guidance and wisdom. He would have the knowledge to guide them through the storms their petty jealousies created, and steer them away from violent altercations. He was fit to rule one of the cities of men. At least the gods thought so. Leeanla still wasn't convinced he was a good choice. For a moment she wondered which city of men he would rule, but the next sound she heard obliterated any curious thoughts about Arkran's future.

"Look," someone said. "Vurl found one."

Vurl. Just hearing his name made Leeanla feel unclean. She looked over to see the boy holding his palm out. Vurl was a few years older than she was, with deep black hair and deep set eyes. He wasn't smiling. He wasn't dancing an excited dance. He just had a cruel twist on his lips. Leeanla had seen that twist before. Nothing good ever came after that twist appeared. This particular curl of his mouth seemed overly nasty.

"What's he doing?"

"He's just looking at it."

Leeanla felt an uncomfortable churning in her stomach. That dark smirk on his lips was a foreboding of something bad about to happen. Something very bad. She took a hesitant step towards him, then another.

Vurl looked up at her approach. He glanced at her left cheek, then back down to the snowflake cupped in his palm. He looked back up and caught her gaze. Leeanla saw his lip curl even more. It was just a slight movement, but it was the ugliest, darkest smile she had ever seen in her life. She looked down at what he held in his palm and her heart seized in her chest. She suddenly found it very hard to breathe.

It was her snowflake. Leeanla instinctively just knew it was hers. "Give it to me, Vurl," she finally managed to say.

Vurl just looked at her. The twisted smile never left his lips. "You've never been very nice to me," he said.

Because you are disgusting. The words burned on her lips, but Leeanla kept them to herself.

Vurl started to curl his hand.

Leeanla heard herself gasp at the threatening movement of his fingers. "It's not yours. The gods meant it for me," she said.

"Did they?" he asked. "Then why is it sitting here in my hand?"

Why was it sitting in his hand? How had that happened? It wasn't supposed to happen that way. "Give it to me, Vurl. It's not yours."

Vurl slowly raised his gaze to meet hers. "Not yet, Leeanla." He shook his head. "Oh, no. Not quite yet."

"Give it to me, Vurl."

Leeanla noticed others started to gather around her and Vurl. A few yards away, Arkran and Katya were still frozen where they stood, still absorbing, assimilating and processing the knowledge of the Ancients.

The look on Vurl's face darkened at the approach of the others. His fingers curled tighter.

"Stay back!" Leeanla raised her arm out to the side. "Stay back!"

The others slowly shuffled to a stop. She could feel their mutterings and murmurings brush past her ears, but she did not hear any of their words. Leeanla focused on the dark, cruel boy in front of her.

Vurl stared at his open palm, rubbing his other hand beneath the back of his palm and his knuckles. He looked up at her. "Sing me a song, Leeanla."

She only stared at him, not certain how to react to that.

"Sing me a song," Vurl said.

"Please, Vurl, don't do this."

Vurl just stared at her. "I know you like to sing. So sing *me* a song."

She slowly raised a hand to Vurl, pointing a slender finger at his cupped palm. "Okay, Vurl. Okay." She opened her mouth, but no song came out; only a crackling nonsensical noise issued from her lips.

"That's not very impressive," Vurl said. He curved his fingers.

Leeanla felt her chest tighten.

"Let's make it a *love* song."

She closed her mouth and swallowed, then licked her lips. She tried again and this time the words started to come out. "I want to be alone with you. I want to be free with you." Her voice cracked and wavered as she sang, but she forced herself to continue on. "I want to share the world with you." Her stomach churned and roiled at the words coming from her mouth. She choked on the next line and couldn't finish it. She couldn't say it, even if the words meant nothing. Not love. No, she just couldn't say it. Not to him. Not to Vurl.

"Go on, finish," Vurl said. "I know the words."

Leeanla narrowed her eyes. "I want to love you," she sang. She fought back a flood of tears that threatened at the corners of her eyes.

"That was pretty crappy," Vurl said. "I don't think

your heart was in it." He shook his head. "I just didn't feel it."

All she could do was stand there. He held her future in the palm of his hand. He held her *eternity* in the palm of his hand.

Vurl looked up at her. "Take off your coat."

Leeanla didn't move.

"Are you really going to make me tell you twice?"

She unbuttoned the first button on her thick woolen coat with shaking fingers. She could feel Vurl's gaze riveting her. She unbuttoned the rest of the buttons.

"Take it off."

Leeanla slid the coat off her shoulders and tossed it to the side. The coat hit the soft snow, sending up a swirling cloud of white sparkling spray. The cold wind hit her, chilling her to her very bones. She grabbed her right arm and rubbed at it.

Vurl devoured her with his gaze. It was as if she could feel his eyes crawling along her face, her chest, her waist, her legs. He purposely lingered at her breasts and at the apex between her legs. His gaze moved back to her breasts. "At least *they* like me," he said with a cruel smirk on his lips.

Leeanla glanced down to see her hardened nipples pushing out against the white fabric of her dress. She looked back up at him but said nothing.

"Or maybe you like me looking at them," Vurl said. "You do, don't you?"

Leeanla fought down the anger simmering inside of her. She bit back a scathing retort and forced a smile to appear on her lips. "Yes, Vurl. I like it when you look at them."

"Ha, I knew it!"

She squeezed her arm tightly, pinching at her skin; the pain in her flesh was a welcome relief to the agony going on inside her head.

"Lift up your dress."

"Vurl," she said.

He glanced down at the snowflake in his palm. "Oh, look. I think it's starting to melt." He looked back up at her. "I'm not sure how long these last, do you? I'm sure at some point it will just melt. Why, it might melt in a few seconds."

She grabbed the fabric of her dress below her waist and started pulling it up. She scrunched the fabric in her hand as she pulled the dress higher and higher. Her calves appeared, then her knees.

Vurl stared with rapt fascination.

Leeanla pulled her dress higher, exposing her thighs to him.

"Oh, those *are* creamy," Vurl said. "They look so soft and smooth."

She hesitated.

"Show it me, Leeanla. Show it me," Vurl whispered. "Everyone says you don't wear anything underneath your dress. I want to see."

And then she showed it to him. She pulled up her dress further, exposing her womanhood to his ravenous gaze.

Vurl beamed a radiant smile. "I knew it. I knew you'd be wild down there. Look at all that hair!" He looked up at her. "That's beautiful, Leeanla. It really is." He glanced back down to stare at the mass of dark hair between her legs.

"Would you like to touch it?" she asked.

Vurl frowned. "What are you, some kind of slut?" And then he did something that had never been done in the entire history of Frawst. He popped the snowflake into his mouth. Her snowflake. Her one chance at achieving unity with the Ancients. Her one chance at reaching the pinnacle of knowledge and wisdom. Her one chance at immortality.

Leeanla could only scream.

She passed by Vurl every morning on her way to the shrine on Alabaster Hill. Every morning she gave him a winsome smile. He never smiled back. So foul-tempered for an immortal, Leeanla thought. You would think living forever would give him something to smile about.

This morning she decided to stop and talk to him. The weather was fine, the wind only slight. "Hello, Vurl."

Vurl said nothing.

Leeanla looked at him thoughtfully. "And how are you enjoying your immortality this bright and sunny morning?"

His sun-cracked lips twitched. They didn't move much, but just enough to let her know that he was listening to her.

"Would you like to see my hairy patch again today?"

Vurl gave her no response, but she knew he was thinking about it. His lips twitched. His gaze shifted from her face, moving down her body.

"Hmm, I bet you would," she said. She raised her wrinkled hand and slowly shook her finger in front of him as she shook her head. "Not today, Vurl, not today." She lowered her hand. "Maybe tomorrow,

Vurl. Maybe tomorrow."

Leeanla continued on her way, waving goodbye with a wrinkled hand. She didn't move as quickly these days. There was a slight hunch to her back, giving her steps a shuffling motion. Her face was weathered and wrinkled with the passing of decades.

Vurl did not wave back, or even pump his fists in outrage. He couldn't. Not without arms. He did not chase after her. He couldn't. Not without legs. He did not shout acidic barbs after her. He couldn't. Not without a tongue. His severed head rested on a stump of ice, on display for all eternity.

Leeanla smiled a soft dark smile. She would visit him again tomorrow and say hello.

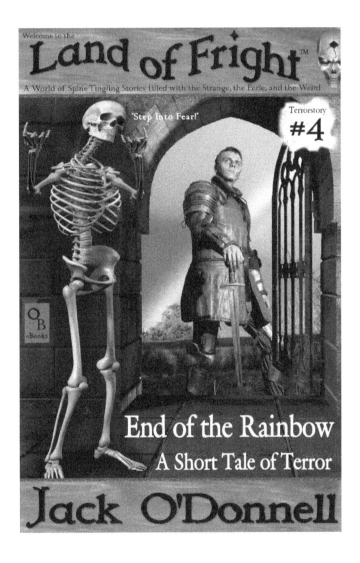

# TERRORSTORY #4
# END OF THE RAINBOW

**"I**'ve never seen one so big."

Galad grinned. He was a big man with a big smile. His back was pressed up against a tree, his breeches down around his ankles. His sword rested up against the tree next to him. The rough tree bark abraded his buttocks, but he didn't mind. The red-haired woman on her knees before him was helping to alleviate that discomfort with her warm lips and stroking fingers. They were taking a well-deserved break from their sparring. Her sword lay on the ground near her knees.

"The rainbow," she said. "The rainbow."

His smile slipped.

"It feels like it's so close. Like we could actually

63

almost find the end of it."

He glanced up at the bright ribbon of color that arced across the sky. Landrial was right. It was the largest rainbow he had ever seen. The colors were vivid, each band of light bright and thick. It nearly filled the entire sky. The end of the rainbow did indeed seem close. Very close.

A half dozen men thundered by on horses, their hooves kicking up tiny clouds of dust as they sped past on the dirt road. One of them pointed at the rainbow and shouted something to the others. Galad couldn't make out the man's words, but the tone was clear; there was an urgency in his voice.

Another man gaped at them as he raced past. He shouted to his fellow riders, pointing back to Galad and Landrial, but no one in the group paid the man any attention. The rest of them were all deeply fixated on the rainbow.

Galad watched them race down the road and disappear around a bend as they headed deeper into the woods. He looked back up at the rainbow. There was something troubling him about it, but he couldn't quite figure out what it was. He stared at the road, at the haze of dust that slowly settled back down to the earth. The sound of the galloping horses faded into the distance.

He turned to look back down at Landrial. She still gripped him in her hand, but it was no longer the focus of her attention. "I think they were thinking the same thing," he said.

Landrial turned her attention back to the matter in hand and licked his member. She looked up at him and grinned.

"The rainbow," he said. "I meant the rainbow."

Landrial studied the empty road for a moment, her gaze traveling the path the riders had taken, then glanced up at the massive rainbow filling the sky. She looked to Galad, anticipation clearly in her eyes.

Galad nodded to her. He eased her fingers from his member and stuffed himself awkwardly away before buttoning up his breeches.

"Don't you want me to finish?" Her green eyes twinkled at him.

"It just gives me something to look forward to." He reached down and caressed the ghost of a scar on her cheek. He still felt guilty about that. He had accidentally cut her a few months ago when they were practicing with their daggers.

"Such self-control," Landrial said with a teasing smile. She rose up and gave him a quick kiss on the lips.

Landrial was a very welcome companion and Galad was glad she decided to give up her life as a tavern wench to join him as he traveled from tournament to tournament. He expected to wake up one day and find her gone, but for now he was going to just enjoy her company. She turned out to be a very capable swordswoman and an excellent sparring partner. She was quite adept at wielding her blade; her quick strikes kept him on his toes. And she was very pleasurable to look it. She had a sensual mouth that had a tendency to utter sharp retorts, but it was a mouth also full of eager passion and he gladly listened to her barbs in exchange for tasting those lips and feeling them on his body.

They quickly gathered up their supplies and stowed them in their packs. Galad grabbed his sword from where it rested up against the tree, swinging it a few times before sliding the blade back into its scabbard.

"What about the tournament?" Landrial asked as she shouldered her leather pack. "We're supposed to be in Northshire before sunset." She sheathed her sword. She jingled the leather pouch tied at her waist. The few meager coins inside barely made a sound. "We're due for some victories."

"There will always be more tournaments." Galad looked up at the rainbow. The bright band of color was incredibly close, as if the shimmering end of it was no more than a quarter mile away. "But I don't think we'll ever see something like this again in our lives."

Landrial nodded.

"They're not there."

"What?"

Galad moved to Landrial's side, sliding down behind the pile of rocks she was hiding behind. Above them, the rainbow filled the sky, arcing down just a few dozen yards from them. He nodded. "They're not there. Just the horses."

"Do you see the end?"

"No. But it's close. Real close. I know it is. There's some kind of weird glow coming from over that next rise."

"Did you see... anything else?"

Galad frowned. "Like what?"

She shrugged. "I don't know." She hesitated for a moment. "Like guards. Like someone watching over it."

"Watching over what?"

"The treasure, you big oaf."

He looked at her, then laughed. "You really believe those stories?"

"Isn't that why we are looking for the end of the rainbow?"

He shook his head. "No. I just wanted to see it." He looked back up at the enormous rainbow towering over them, then looked back at her. "You really thought we were hunting down a treasure?"

Landrial looked away, her face flushing as nearly as red as her hair.

"Maybe it's guarded by ferocious leprechauns, too," he said.

She looked at him. "Yeah, maybe. Ever heard of anybody surviving a fight with a ferocious leprechaun?"

"No, can't say that I have."

She nodded. "Exactly. That's why nobody's ever gotten their hands on the treasure." She paused. "Those ferocious leprechauns win every fight."

Galad was quiet for a long moment. "Maybe you are right, though," he said. "Maybe there really is a treasure. Those old stories always have some grain of truth to them somewhere in the tale." He shook his head. "Doesn't matter. I still want to see it."

She nodded. "Me, too."

They sat in silence for a moment.

"There are six men down there," she finally said.

"I counted five."

Landrial shook her head. "Six. You probably forgot to count the one who was pointing to your big dick in my hand." She reached over and put her hand on his crotch.

"I was a bit distracted," he said. He leaned over and gave her a sweet kiss on her lips.

She playfully pushed him away. "Ah ah. Not now. We've got to concentrate on getting past those men."

Galad nodded and fingered the hilt of his sword. "And maybe some ferocious leprechauns. It'll be good practice for the next tournament." He motioned for Landrial to follow him. "We can't go this way. We'll spook the horses. Let's circle around."

⋘⋙

And there it was. The end of the rainbow. Or was it the beginning? No matter. It was a sight to behold. The individual lines of colors were thick and vibrant. Red orange yellow green blue purple. All gleaming and glowing with an unearthly shimmer.

But the colored streams of light that arced up into the sky were not what riveted Galad's gaze. Nor was it the huge black pot with a thick black rim situated at the end of the rainbow; it was larger than any other pot he had ever seen, much more akin to a giant cauldron than a pot. What demanded his attention was the pile of gold amassed around the cauldron. It was just like the stories had said. Galad couldn't believe it. All the old tales were true. All that glittering gold strewn about the ground was enough to pull his gaze away from the rainbow and away from the huge black cauldron.

"Wow," Landrial said.

Galad glanced at her.

She shrugged. "That's all I got. Just wow."

They waited and watched, crouched behind a fallen tree. They watched and waited. The gold nuggets glistened and glittered. They saw no movement. They listened. They heard nothing but the soft shuffling sounds of animals nearby and the soft cries of birds in the trees. The gold gleamed and glinted.

"That's a lot of gold," Landrial said.

Galad just nodded. He continued to scan the area. He glanced over his shoulder, then back to Landrial. "See anything?"

She shook her head, keeping her gaze riveted on the gold. "Where are they?" Landrial asked. "They wouldn't just leave their horses like that."

"No, they wouldn't." Galad was silent for a moment. "Any sign of ferocious leprechauns?" He meant it as a joke, but there was a serious tone to the question when it came out of his mouth.

Landrial's lips quirked into a grin. She shook her head. She looked away from the gold and did a quick scan of their surroundings. "You see any?"

"No. I don't see anything."

They watched quietly for another few moments. The end of the rainbow shimmered less than a stone's throw away. They could see the men's horses tied to trees in the far distance. But there was no sign of the men at all. The ground was covered with a tangled mass of leaves and grass and plants, making it hard to discern whether anything had been disturbed in the area lately or not.

"Let's go closer," Galad finally said. He put his hand on his sword handle and rose up.

Galad looked at the end of the rainbow. It wasn't

coming out of the cauldron like he had first thought; it was situated just beyond it. The rainbow looked like it was actually touching the ground, rising up out of the earth. The colors shimmered and glistened with a wet sheen. It was hard to tell if the rainbow had real physical substance to it or if it was just purely beams of light.

There was still no sign of the six men. Their horses whinnied in the distance; a few of them bucked, trying to get free, but their reins were expertly wrapped around tree trunks and they couldn't escape their bindings.

Galad and Landrial slowly approached the end of the rainbow. Gold nuggets glittered on the ground, leading up to the huge cauldron. He reached a piece of gold and stooped to pick it up. He turned it over in his hand. It looked like gold, but it had an odd weight to it. It was too light. He looked over to see Landrial studying the gold as well. "This feels strange," he said to her.

Landrial held a few nuggets in her hand. She took out a small blade and put the sharp tip to one of the nuggets, pressing against it. The blade easily pierced the surface. "Ugh," she said. "It's too soft." She lifted the nuggets to her nose and sniffed. Her face wrinkled in disgust. "That's foul." She let the nuggets drop to the ground and re-sheathed her blade. She glanced around the area, wiping her hand on her breeches as her gaze scanned their surroundings. "I'm still worried about those men. Where did they go?"

"I'm more worried about who put out this fake gold," Galad said. He sniffed the nugget and immediately grimaced at the smell. The stench when he held it up close to his nose was worse than fresh horse dung. What the hell was it? He looked again at the nugget, then tossed it aside. He had no idea what it was. It certainly wasn't gold.

He slowly neared the large big black cauldron. The top rim of the huge cauldron reached up to his chest; the entire pot was about a dozen feet wide. He moved closer and glanced inside. The hairs on the back of his neck bolted upright.

He had found the men.

"Run, Landrial!" Galad screamed. "Run! There's no treasure. It's a trap. It's a trap!"

That's when a dazzling white light appeared from the end of the rainbow, rising up out of the ground. It moved with purpose, a shape with form and substance. It was unlike any earthly creature he had ever seen. He couldn't make out its true form; the white light was too bright to look at. The rainbow moved as if it were somehow attached to the creature, flowing out of its back like some massively monstrous tail.

Galad drew his sword, gripping it with both hands, readying himself to fight. This was no ferocious leprechaun. This was something far worse. The rainbow itself was some type of unearthly beast.

"Galad, what the hell is that?"

The creature moved straight for Landrial, grabbing her in some kind of unbreakable embrace of light. It was on her before she could swing her dagger, pinning her arms to her sides with two thick bands of light that surrounded her body. Galad could hear her flesh sizzle where the creature touched her. She opened her mouth to cry out but a tentacle of light burst out of the creature and immediately suffocated her as it filled the space between her lips. Any moisture in her mouth immediately burned away; dozens of cracks exploded onto her lips and started to bleed.

Galad bolted over to her, swinging savagely at the creature's back. The sword moved harmlessly through it, the blade glowing intensely as it moved through the creature's white hot body. "Landrial!"

A thick tentacle of white light erupted out of the creature. It lashed out at Galad, striking him across the face and neck, the force of the blow knocking him back away from the creature, sending him crashing to the ground. His flesh burned where the tentacle had struck him.

Landrial only struggled for a brief moment before she fell silent forever. The creature withdrew the tentacle from her body, sliding the thick strand of light up and out of her throat and mouth. Her flesh smoked. The creature lifted her off the ground with its tentacle-like appendages and dumped her unceremoniously into the large cauldron to join the mangled bodies of the six men.

"Landrial!"

The creature turned to face Galad as he moved back to his feet. Were those eyes? Galad couldn't tell. The face, if what he was looking at was a face, kept shifting, altering, the angles and lines changing constantly. His brain couldn't comprehend what he was looking at. It had somewhat of a human shape, but it kept changing, with an arm appearing in one place, then what looked like a leg appearing somewhere else. There were tiny sparks of light bursting in mini eruptions all over its body.

Galad raised his sword but the creature was on him in an instant, squeezing him with its thick tentacles. His arms and chest flared with fiery pain. Two tendrils burst out of the creature, zeroing in on his eyes, penetrating them, sending white hot bolts of light straight into his brain. He squeezed his eyes shut tight but couldn't stop the light from piercing him. He couldn't stop the creature from penetrating his entire being. Galad dropped his sword as he felt himself swelling; it felt as if his entire body was expanding at a rapid rate. Then the white radiance vanished, replaced by a deep darkness.

A white shape hovered over the black cauldron. Galad struggled to clear his vision. He was still alive. The creature stood at the edge of the black cauldron, its faceless face peering down at him. The rainbow was still visible, growing out of its back like a massive fin from hell. Then the rainbow growing out of the creature's back started to dwindle, becoming smaller, shrinking back into its body. As the rainbow shrank back into the creature, the white coloring of the monster started to darken. It was absorbing the rainbow back into itself, absorbing the colored stream of light.

Galad blinked rapidly, forcing his eyes to focus. His entire body felt like it was on fire. His stomach felt like boiling water was bubbling inside of it. How the hell am I still alive? Above him, through the haze of this nightmare, he watched the rainbow slowly vanish, becoming smaller, thinner. Soon, the creature had no color to it at all and only the outline of a pitch black shape was visible. The rainbow was gone, pulled back into the creature's body.

He felt odd lumps beneath him, digging into his back, his legs. Galad knew what they were. The bodies of the other men. And Landrial. He was laying on top of Landrial. He wanted to shout, but all that came out was a grunt. He could barely breathe. He groped the area around his hand for his sword, any sword, any weapon, but when he touched someone's cold face he stopped. He lay still, struggling for a breath.

Galad finally realized what had been troubling him before. The ground was not wet when the riders had ridden past them. There had been no rain. The rainbow had just appeared out of a clear blue sky. He should have known something wasn't right about it. He should have known.

He heard something that sounded like lips smacking together obscenely. A black shape hovered over the cauldron. His vision blurred, then came into focus again. There was movement in the black shape, like a seam being split. Galad gazed up at the biggest, whitest, sharpest looking teeth he had ever seen. They looked like the jagged edges of a portcullis. "I've never seen one so big," he heard a voice say.

And then Galad heard nothing ever again.

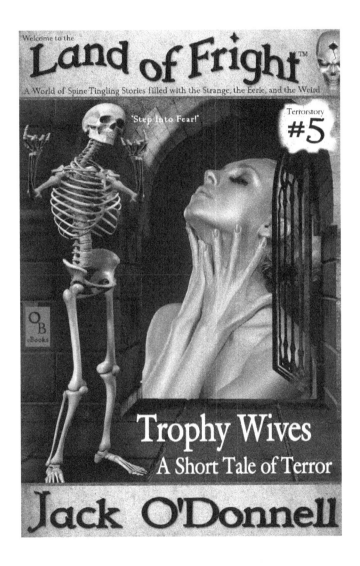

# TERRORSTORY #5
# TROPHY WIVES

**"I** like **to call them my trophy wives."**

"Were you married to all of them?"

"Oh, heavens no. I just like to call them that."

"Were you married to any of them?"

"No."

Tiffany Valanday looked at him curiously for a moment, but said nothing. She was a slender woman with thick blonde hair and a fair complexion. The gentle blue color of her dress complemented her deep blue eyes. She clutched her small purse as she moved through the room. Her nails were long and fashionably painted with a soft floral design.

Jonathan Franks pointed to an empty bronze pedestal. "I have a new piece coming in."

"You do?"

He nodded. "In fact, real soon." His lips twitched with a knowing smile. "It's called *TV Time*."

Tiffany glanced at Jonathan. He was a thin man with a receding hairline and a pencil-thin mustache that just looked absurd on his face. She fought back the urge to lick her finger and wipe it off his skin. But he did exude an oddly compelling confidence. There was something alluring about him, she had to admit. Perhaps it was because of his wealth. He just radiated money. It certainly wasn't because of his looks.

She turned back to study the room. They were standing in his penthouse along Lake Shore Drive in Chicago. Outside the massive window at the far end of the large room, the night sky was beginning to deepen. Lake Michigan was visible, the moonlight softly glowing on its surface. The room was dotted with dozens of statues situated on pedestals of different heights and widths, all of them nude human shapes in various poses. Each statue was skillfully lit by several expertly placed spotlights. "They are so life like."

"Thank you." Jonathan gave her a slight bow. "I try to grab a moment out of time that best represents their life. It takes great effort to capture their true essence when I create them."

"Why don't you just use a camera?"

Jonathan grimaced and grunted. "I'm no good with all that digital mumbo jumbo. F-stops and apertures and lenses. Not for me. I need to touch and feel. I want to capture time in solid form." He reached out and stroked a statue of a nude woman cast in bronze. The figure was standing tall, her arms at her sides, her head raised as if looking off into the distance. He ran the backs of his fingers along her ample chest, pausing for the briefest of moments on an erect nipple before sliding his fingers past it. "And a sculpture lasts longer than a photo."

Tiffany looked over to a statue on a wider lower pedestal situated nearby. Her high heels clacked softly on the wooden floor of the cavernous room as she walked over to it. The gold sculpture was of a naked woman on her hands and knees, looking back over her shoulder. A small spotlight illuminated her slightly parted lips, her lidded eyes. Her curvaceous rear was slightly tilted, obviously eager. Another spotlight shone on the folds of her womanhood.

"Rather crude, isn't it?"

Jonathan joined her. "Is it? One of my favorites, really. There is something quite exciting about a woman locked in the throes of desire, isn't there? Something about that look in her eyes, that slightly parted mouth." He awkwardly adjusted himself.

Tiffany didn't respond.

"And she did like it doggie-style," he mused. He patted the statue on the head. "She liked it very much."

Tiffany moved on to the next sculpture. It was an elderly woman sitting in a bathtub. Her eyes were closed, her face scrunched tight, her head resting back up against the rim. Her saggy breasts were mostly hidden below the metal that simulated the smooth surface of water. The fingers on her right hand gripped the edge of the tub with a very tight grip. The old woman looked like she was hanging on for dear life. Tiffany looked at her without comment and moved on.

Jonathan quietly followed her, keeping a few steps behind her.

"So the statues at the art show, what were those?"

He waved his hand nonchalantly. "Oh, those were my throw aways. I just create those to make money. These are my true treasures. I wouldn't sell any of them."

"It's amazing how far you've come. First, your golden insects, then cats and dogs. Now, these."

He smiled proudly at her. "Ahh, you've read up on me."

She nodded. "Of course. Whenever I attend a show I like to learn as much about the artist as I can. Makes their works seem all the more — impressive somehow. So many of them have had troubled pasts. It's amazing what many of them overcome on their journeys to becoming real artists." She waited for him to respond, wondering if he would reveal more about his checkered past, but he didn't take the bait. She knew he had been in trouble with the law before, but she wasn't able to find any specifics.

Tiffany moved on to the next statue. It was a golden statue of a nude woman sitting in a chair reading a book.

"She so loved her paperbacks," Jonathan said. "Stephen King was a favorite. She refused to even use the Kindle I bought her. So old fashioned. She liked to feel the paper in her hands. She liked to hear the pages crinkle when she turned them."

Tiffany studied the nude golden woman for a moment. "Why gold?"

"Why indeed. I'm trying to elevate gold out of the clutches of trinket makers. It is worthy of so much more than vulgar baubles and mere practical objects, don't you think?"

Tiffany fingered the gold necklace she wore. "I do

like my gold."

Jonathan's expression softened. "And it likes you."

She smiled at him.

"I will admit I prefer mixing a bit of bronze alloy in with the gold," he said. "The bronze expands slightly before it sets, highlighting all those exquisite details."

She nodded and continued moving amongst the statues. She pointed to a golden sculpture of a woman on a black pedestal. "Did you capture her essence?"

Jonathan nodded. "Of course. She's one of my favorites."

Tiffany moved closer to the statue. Several tiny spotlights situated far above the statue illuminated the figure's wide eyes. "Was she always this scared?" She stroked the metal woman's cheek, running her slender fingers over her golden lips, her scream-frozen mouth.

Jonathan stared at the statue. Tiffany could see a slight hint of a smile cross over on his lips, and then it was gone. "Not always," he said.

"And this is how you wanted to remember her?"

He shook his head. "It doesn't matter how I *wanted* to remember her. That is just how— the piece came out. I can't change the essence of my subjects. I can only capture it."

Tiffany stared at the statue's wide eyes, the tautness of the golden woman's face. "She looks like she's in pain."

"Not anymore."

"Did she pose like this? That must have been difficult for her to hold that position for very long."

He nodded. "It was difficult for her." He paused. "It was difficult for both of us. But that's why I think it turned out so well. Sometimes, the hardest things we do turn out to be the best things we do, don't you agree?"

She didn't answer. She slowly pulled her hand away from the sculpture. "Where is she now?"

"Once I finish a work, I never hear from a subject again."

"Never?"

Jonathan looked straight at her. "Never."

Tiffany was quiet for a moment. She looked back at him. "Do you only work with nudes?"

He nodded. "I find them easier to handle. Clothes just get in the way of their true nature."

Tiffany turned to him. "Would you like to see me nude?" She pushed a stray lock of her blonde hair back behind her ear.

He stared at her. "The thought had occurred to me, yes."

She pursed her lips, nodded and turned away. "Is that why you invited me up here?"

He hesitated, but only for a brief moment. "Yes."

She shook her head. "I don't think so. I'd make a poor subject. I can never sit still."

"My dear Tiffany, you don't need to sit still." He reached out and took her fingers into his hand. "I just need to observe you for a while. Be with you. Take you to dinner. Take you to a concert. Take you to Paris. See you at work. See you at play. Then I can capture your essence."

She glanced down to where he held her hand, then looked back up at him. "And you think I would enjoy Paris?"

"I think Paris would certainly enjoy you."

"Gold and Paris. I'm starting to accumulate a lot

of admirers." She smiled.

"Yes, you are."

"But if you add me to your collection, you'll never speak to me again." There was a disappointed pouty lilt in her voice. She eased her hand away from him. "You just said so."

Jonathan raised a finger and opened his mouth as if about to correct her, but then paused. He lowered his hand. "Perhaps you'll be the exception to the rule."

Tiffany smiled at him. "Perhaps I will be." She glanced down at his hand, then reached out to take his fingers into hers. She looked back up at him. "You would really take me to Paris?"

"Of course. We can leave whenever you want. I don't have another show for a few months."

Tiffany was quiet for a moment. "I would need to pack a few things."

He nodded. "After I take you to dinner."

"So tell me how you work," Tiffany said. "I find the work habits of artists and writers incredibly fascinating."

"Is that why you were at the art expo? Collecting stories of work habits?" Jonathan took a bite of his ribeye steak, chewing it slowly and deliberately.

A waiter paused at their table and re-filled Tiffany's water glass. She nodded at him and gave him a quick smile. She took a sip from the water, then looked at Jonathan over the rim of the glass. "I guess you could say that." She set the glass down. "So how do you choose who your next model will be? How do you know they are the *right* one? How do you decide they are the one to focus all your effort on?"

He pointed his steak knife at her. "Good question. It might seem like a pat answer, but I just know who my next subject will be the moment I see her."

"You just know?"

He nodded. "As soon as I see her, I know."

"What, like some kind electrical charge you get in your brain? The proverbial light bulb going off in your head?"

Jonathan shrugged. "I just know."

"So is the light bulb going off now?" She pursed her lips with a slight movement.

He looked at her. "With a blinding glare."

Tiffany reached under the table and put her hand on his thigh. "Anything else getting a charge?"

He glanced around the room, then looked at her. "I prefer to play those games in private."

She slowly eased her hand from his leg. She took another drink of water. "What if your next model refuses? What if the light bulb goes off but she doesn't want to play?"

"I really don't know. It's never happened."

"What if it did?"

He paused. "Why would they refuse? That would make no sense."

"What if I refuse?" Tiffany asked.

"That would also make no sense. You have a once in a lifetime opportunity to be immortalized in gold and you would say *no thank you*?"

She shrugged. "Maybe I just don't have the time."

Jonathan smiled a knowing smile. "Ahh, it's all about time, isn't it? That unstoppable beast. That juggernaut that just keeps rolling along and squashing everything in its path. That's what I'm fighting in my work."

She looked at him with a slight narrowing of her eyes. "You can't beat time."

He waved his knife in the air, motioning to the room around them. "Not out here, no. Not in this world." He lowered his hand. "But in my world, in my work, I grab a little piece of life and freeze it. I stop it and make it solid before time can wither it and kill it."

"That gives you a sense of satisfaction, doesn't it?"

He set his knife down on his plate and leaned back in his chair. "Immense satisfaction. Every piece I create is a victory against time."

Tiffany was quiet for a moment. "I didn't see any molds or sculpting tools in your studio."

He shook his head. "I don't create them there. I have a special place where I make them. I like to call it my secret laboratory."

"Why? Are you a mad scientist?"

Jonathan laughed a very hearty laugh. "A scientist, no? Mad, yes." He laughed again.

"Will you show it to me?"

He shook his head. "I don't show it to anybody." He raised his knife. "Except of course to those women who agree to be one of my subjects."

Tiffany cocked her head curiously at him. "You like that word, don't you? Subjects. You are the king and all your trophy wives serve you." She eased off one of her high heels and rubbed her stockinged foot against his leg.

He shrugged. "An artist has needs."

The waiter stopped at their table. "Would the gentleman and the lady care for some dessert? We have decadent chocolate cake or perhaps a piece of delicious apple pie slathered with caramel drippings."

Jonathan glanced at Tiffany and she shook her head softly. She fingered the gold pendant that hung between her breasts, drawing his gaze to her chest. He looked back up at the waiter. "No, we're going to have our dessert elsewhere."

"I thought you had to pack a few things."

"Not yet. Take your pants off."

There was a brief moment of silence. "Now?"

"Now. I'm ready. Aren't you?"

"It must have been all that talk of pie and drippings," he quipped.

Tiffany reached up and caressed his cheek. "No, just you," she said. "Now get those pants off."

A rustling of clothes signaled his acquiescence to her command.

"Sit here," she said.

"Can't you turn some lamps on?" Jonathan asked. The light was murky in Tiffany's apartment; only their vague dark outlines were visible in the dim light coming from some small windows nearby.

"I will. Not yet." Tiffany grabbed his hand and tugged him down onto the chair. She brushed against his manhood. "You are eager, aren't you?" A soft laugh bubbled from her lips.

"Eager for your beaver."

The laughter quickly stopped. "Oh, you *are* crude." Jonathan was silent.

"Put your hands behind the chair."

He did.

She wrapped a thick coarse rope around his wrists, binding them behind the back of the chair.

"I'm not sure if I like this," he said.

"You can't always be in charge, can you? A man like you needs to let go once in a while. Let someone else do all the work." Tiffany reached down and stroked his manhood. "*He* certainly likes it," she cooed.

Jonathan moaned with pleasure, then groaned with disappointment when she let go.

"I really have to show you *my* collection," she said. "You are probably one of the few men who would really appreciate it. Ha, you actually might be the *only* one who would appreciate it."

"You are a collector?"

Tiffany sighed. "I'm disappointed. Is that how you see me? Just a collector of other's art?" She shook her head. "No, I am an artist, as you are."

"A fellow artist? Now I am truly intrigued. You didn't mention that at dinner."

"I can't tell you all my secrets right away, now can I?" Tiffany reached down and stroked him again, moving her hand up and down him, stroking him faster and faster.

Jonathan nodded. "Yes, yes. I do want to see your collection."

"First things first. Let's get you as long and hard as we can."

"Yes, please do." His breath quickened.

She gripped him, stroked him, felt him harden and lengthen in her hand. "There's a special place I want to put this."

Jonathan moaned. "Oh, yes. Let's put it in your special place."

A light suddenly flared hotly to life.

And his eyes went wide.

The room was ringed with pedestals and shelves. Pedestals and shelves full of small statues. Statues of very recognizable objects.

"Do you like my collection?"

Jonathan found himself unable to speak as he took in the sights that surrounded him. They were all statues of penises. Statues of bronzed cocks. Statues of silver cocks. Statues of gold cocks. Penises of all different shapes and sizes filled shelves and tables all around him. One thick gold cock was situated on a shelf just to his right. A row of bronze penises filled a shelf on the wall to his left. Several silver cocks were artfully displayed on their own pedestal stand just a dozen feet in front of him.

"I have a new piece coming in," Tiffany said.

And then something else drew his gaze. A framed picture on a nearby desk. It was a picture of a smiling, contented woman. A woman he recognized. A woman he had immortalized in gold. A woman with a permanent scream captured in cold metal.

A smell hit Jonathan's nose and he cursed himself for not recognizing it earlier. It was the smell of molten metal.

"In fact, real soon," Tiffany said. "I'm going to call it *Sister's Revenge*. But, unlike you, I only need to capture a part of my subject. In your case, a very small part."

She raised her hand and he saw the silvery glint of a carving knife.

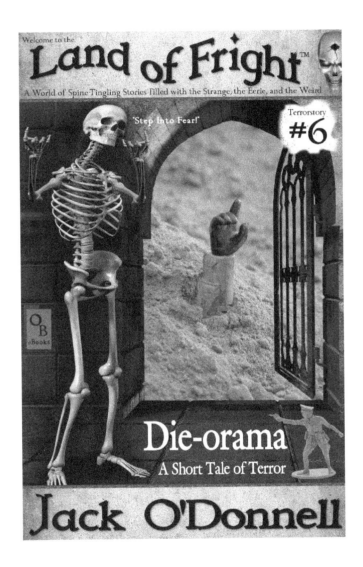

# TERRORSTORY #6
# DIE-ORAMA

Carlton Jones knew where he was and it scared the living shit out of him. Which was a much more terrifying feeling than getting the dead shit scared out of you, he thought with a wry amusement that wasn't at all appropriate for the position he was in. He wasn't amused at all. He didn't even know what living shit was, but the thought had flashed through his mind the moment he realized what he was looking at. Bottom line: he was fucked.

He was standing in ankle high grass on the edge of a cobblestone road. But the grass wasn't real; they were just tufts of old chopped up toothbrushes painted to look like grass and shoved into a base of celluclay. The road wasn't real either; that surface was made of large clump cat litter speckled with varying shades of brown and red paint to give it a cobblestone appearance.

*"Get to the other side and you will live."*

That's what that fucker had said to him.

It sounded easy enough. Except Carlton knew what he had to get past to reach the other side. And that's what really freaked him out. Because if *he* could move inside this diorama, then so could *they*.

The burnt out husk of a Sherman tank was off to his right. Beyond that, several partially demolished buildings lined the right side of the cobblestone street. And beyond that, behind the buildings, there was nothing but deep blackness. It was a wall of black just like the wall of black right behind him. It was impenetrable. For all intents and purposes, it was the end of the world. It was certainly the end of his world.

Carlton looked down at the dark pants covering his legs, the heavy black boots on his feet. The fucker had dressed him like a soldier straight out of a World War II movie. 'Cept his story was called Saving Carlton Jones. He thought of the guy undressing him and his skin crawled. Who knows what else that demented fucker did to him when he had him naked. He shuddered.

He looked up into the fake blue sky above him. "It was just a fucking battery for my RC car! Shit, man, I'll pay you for it!"

Were those huge eyes staring down at him? Carlton wasn't sure, but it looked like two massive eyes were looking down at him with grim amusement.

He raised his fist to the sky and shook his hand.

The world shook back.

Carlton felt his vision dim and then everything went black.

His eyes opened and suddenly everything looked real. Very real. The burnt out husk of the Sherman was now smoking, a white haze drifting up from its shattered bulk. The street was a cobblestone road. The grass was real. The ruins of stores and homes that dotted the street were real. Carlton noticed several bodies near the tank. They were GIs. And they looked all too real. From the grotesque angles of their bodies, he was certain they were dead. *Dead!* His mind screamed. *How could they be dead? They are just pieces of plastic! How is this possible? How can I be in this place?*

A reflection caught his eye in the distance, a bright flash of light, and he moved towards a house that had its front wall blown to bits. There was a hallway mirror a few feet inside the living room, just beyond a torn up couch. He stepped over the rubble of the wall and moved into the room.

Carlton looked at himself in the shattered mirror and he felt his own thoughts shatter in a spider web of panic. He was dressed as a Nazi SS officer. He even had half a dozen metals sewn on his chest. One of them was the Knight's Iron Cross or some shit. He pulled at the shirt but felt his skin pulling along with it. He yanked harder and felt his flesh tear. It was glued on. The fucker had glued a Nazi uniform onto his skin.

He glanced up at the building at the far end of the diorama. A flag fluttered in the breeze. Carlton didn't know how a breeze could be blowing inside the diorama, but it was. The Nazi flag was fluttering, the swastika big and black on the red background.

Movement caught his eye to his right and he quickly rolled back around the corner, pinning himself to the wall. His right hand brushed something hard and cold at his side. He glanced down to see a Luger resting in a holster at his waist. He reached for it, but then stopped, afraid for a moment the weapon wouldn't move, afraid that it was glued into the holster. But when he grabbed the handle and pulled, the Luger slid out easily into his hand. He smiled a grim smile as he studied the brown wood grip, the sleek black metal, the narrow barrel, then slid the gun back into its holster.

A flash of olive drab cloth in the corner of his vision made his heart seize in his chest. He knew what that was. American soldiers were most likely in the diorama with him. He moved farther down the wall, away from where he had seen the glimpse of GI clothing. *Maybe I should surrender,* he thought. *Plead for mercy.* Then he remembered the dead American soldiers near the tank. Carlton was pretty certain every GI he encountered would shoot first and ask questions later. *Hell, they wouldn't even ask questions of a guy in a Nazi uniform. They would just shoot.*

Carlton peered around the corner, eyeing the fluttering Nazi flag atop the building in the distance a few blocks away. He could see the steps leading up to the dark doorway. It looked so close, but he had no idea how many soldiers were between him and his escape. He also knew he couldn't just stand still. He had to move.

Carlton peeked over the remains of the crumbled

wall again. *Fuck*. There were only three bodies near the smoking Sherman tank. He was positive he had seen four bodies before. One of them obviously wasn't dead. He lowered himself back down behind the wall. How many of them were out there?

A bullet pinged off the wall inches from his head, showering him with bits of brick. He whipped his head around to see an American GI aiming down the sights of his M1 Garand rifle.

Carlton sprang up, rolling up over the shattered wall, getting on the opposite side of the wall from the GI. Another two rounds slammed against the bricks, sending more shattered pieces of wall flying in all directions.

He scanned the area in front of him. There were two demolished houses to his right. They would provide plenty of cover but there was a stretch of open ground about forty feet wide before he would reach them. The cobblestone street was littered with debris, shattered pieces of wood, piles of rubble. He noticed a hand reaching up out of the rubble, its fingers pointed skyward. *Nice touch, you sick fucker.* The fingers wiggled. The pile of debris on top of the person shifted.

*Shit, time to move.* Carlton looked to his left and saw an overturned jeep about a dozen feet away. It was in the opposite direction of the building he needed to reach, but it was the only choice he had. Jerry cans were scattered around the vehicle. One of the drab olive metal cans was marked with a big white X. He knew that symbol designated a water can. Carlton licked his lips, suddenly feeling very thirsty, but he pushed the thought away. He moved into a crouched position, ready to spring forward towards the jeep. He glanced down and pick up a loose chunk of rock. He took a deep breath, tossed the rock to his right, then bolted left, bursting out from behind the wall, bolting for the cover of the overturned jeep.

He heard a ricochet behind him as a round skipped off the cobblestone road. He neared the jeep and ducked around it, hearing a loud metallic clang just above his head as he rounded the vehicle. *Shit, that was close. Too fucking close.* He struggled to catch his breath, leaning hard against the metal side of the jeep. *Was that five shots?* he wondered. He wasn't sure. He knew the Garand held eight bullets in a clip, but he wasn't sure how many rounds the GI had fired off.

Carlton pulled the Luger out of its holster. The gun felt cool in his hand, the wood grip cold against his skin. He studied the weapon. *Did it have a safety?* It looked like there was one on the top rear of the gun, a small lever. *Was the safety off when the lever was up or down? Fuck.* He had no idea. *It's gotta be down.* He flicked the lever down. He fought the urge to fire the weapon to be sure. He knew the sound would give his position away. *Fuck, they already know where I am. I need to know if this thing will shoot.*

He spotted a stray jerry can off to the side of the road. He aimed and pulled at the trigger. The trigger was locked. *Fuck, it's up.* He flipped the safety switch up, then took aim again. The Luger fired and the recoil took him off guard, shoving his hand back towards him, the toggle action pushing the gun slightly downward. The empty brass popped up and out of the gun, nearly hitting him in the face. The bullet hit something with a clattering sound, but nowhere near where he was aiming. *Shit, I suck.* Carlton gripped the Luger tighter, holding it with both hands. He fired off another shot, braced for the recoil. This time, the bullet careened off the ground near the jerry can, only missing it by a few feet. He gripped the gun tighter, took careful aim, and fired again. The bullet hit the ground inches from the jerry can, but hit the side of it as it careened off the ground. He smiled a tight smile at the satisfying clink of metal being struck.

Another bullet hit the jeep, clanging off the metal. Carlton startled, ducking down into a tight crouch. *Keep moving, you idiot.* He looked off to his left at the two houses nearby. They were in decent shape, their walls nearly fully intact. Their door were closed, but one of them had a shattered front window. He crept forward to the edge of the jeep, moving as close as he could to the houses while still maintaining cover. He eyed the opening in the window. It was definitely big enough for him to fit through.

He went for it, bursting out from behind the jeep, charging towards the window. He neared the window and dove forward just as the remaining fragment of window shattered from a bullet strike from the GI's Garand. Slivers of glass bounced off his Nazi uniform as he soared through the opening. He hit the ground awkwardly and felt a sharp pain in his right shoulder. He lost his grip on the Luger and the weapon skirted along the tiled floor.

Carlton moved to his knees, fumbling in the dim light for his gun. Shards of glass bit into his left palm but he ignored the stinging pain. He saw the Luger against the back wall and crawled over to it. He exhaled a sharp grunt of relief as he clutched the weapon. He leaned back up against the wall, still breathing hard. His left palm was dotted with blood; a few small fragments of glass stuck out of his skin. He brushed them off and some more blood spots appeared on his flesh.

He looked up and realized he was clearly visible through the window frame. He darted to the side and moved in a crouch up to the window, keeping to the left. He took a cautious glance outside. His right shoulder ached but he did his best to ignore the pain.

The Sherman tank was still emitting a thin trail of smoke. The three bodies were still motionless. The other GI was nowhere in sight. The Nazi flag flapped in the breeze, taunting him with the hope of escape.

Carlton struggled to remember the layout of the diorama, but he couldn't bring in any details to his mind. The fucker had shown it to him when he had first come into the hobby store, but he didn't pay any attention to it. *Did these houses on this side of the street reach up to the office building at the end of the street?* Maybe he could move through them. He looked to his right and saw a doorway. He cast a quick glance out the window.

The GI stood a few feet away, his rifle at the ready.

Carlton shrieked and ducked as the soldier fired. He heard the round whizz right past his ear. Then he heard the tell-tale *ping* of the eight-round clip being ejected from the Garand. The GI was out of ammo! Carlton rose and fired off three shots from his Luger. He didn't even know where the first bullet went because he didn't even aim it, but he was pretty certain the second and third bullets hit the GI square in the chest. The soldier just crumpled to the ground.

Carlton kept the Luger aimed at the fallen man, gripping the gun tightly with two hands. He waited for a long moment, watching for any sign of movement, but the soldier remained still. Dark splotches were visible on the GI's uniform as the blood continued to seep out of the two holes in his chest. Carlton took a few cautious steps closer, the Luger aimed squarely at the GI's chest. He neared the body and stopped, staring down.

For a moment, Carlton felt a surge of disgust at himself. He just shot a GI. They were his favorite heroes in all of history. No one was more noble, more heroic than a World War II GI fighting for the world's freedom. *Fuck! It was him or me. I had to do it.*

The Nazi flag flapped, drawing his gaze. And he realized he was standing in the middle of the street, with open space all around him. He moved, racing back to the shattered window of the house. He stepped through the window and moved quickly to the open doorway he had seen earlier. It led to another room in the house, but it was a dead end; there were no other doors or windows. *Shit.* He wasn't going to be able to move through the houses to get to the office building. He turned around and returned to the window, stepping back over it.

For a moment, he stood just outside the shattered window, studying his surroundings. He turned to look to his right. The office building was maybe half a block away, but there was no cover at all between the end of the houses and the stairs leading up to the building.

Carlton heard a sound of movement coming from behind him. He whirled around to see a woman stumbling towards him. Her once-white dress was stained with dirt and oil and blood. Her dark hair was matted, her face streaked with dark splotches of grime and mud. Her fingers were curled at her waist, red with rivulets of blood. It was the body he had seen under the rubble. He was sure of it. She stopped as she saw him looking at her. "Help—"

A shot from the Luger cut off her plea, jerking her body back as the bullet struck her shoulder. *Fuck that, I am not dealing with that zombie.* She isn't a zombie, a dissenting voice whispered in his head. She spoke. *Too fucking bad. She ain't speakin' no more.*

Carlton fired again.

Carlton reached the last house and hugged the wall, pinning his back tight against the brick. He peered around the corner. There it was, the door! Up a flight of about three dozen steps. So close, yet so far. There was a stretch of cobblestone road he had to cross. There was zero cover. No rubble, no burnt out husk of a jeep or a tank to hide behind.

He re-gripped the Luger, tightening his fingers around the handle. He closed his eyes for a brief moment, then exploded out from the wall, pushing himself off the brick with a violent lunge. He sped over the cobblestone road, expecting to hear gunfire, expecting bullets to chip up the road as they whizzed past him, expecting the sharp bite of a slug in his back.

But none of that happened.

Carlton reached the front sidewalk of the building, then raced up the steps, a jubilant feeling swelling up in his head. He could hear the Nazi flag flapping above him as he leaped up two steps at a time. He was going to make it out of this insane hell-hole!

"Going somewhere, bub?"

Carlton looked up to see a GI stepping out of the dark doorway. The soldier clutched a Thompson sub-machine gun at his waist, the barrel aimed directly at his chest.

Carlton brought up the Luger and pulled at the trigger. Only then did he see that the slide toggle was up and locked open; the gun was empty. Click.

Carlton only had a few seconds to take in the American soldier's sergeant stripes, his stubbled beard, the cocked angle of his helmet, before he noticed the GI's finger tighten on the trigger.

"Man, this is cool. That's some pretty realistic battle damage. Those bullet holes are pretty slick."

Xander Simonsen smiled at the customer standing at the counter in his hobby shop. He watched the man turn the Nazi figure over and over in his hands as he studied it. Xander was a well-dressed man in his late fifties, sporting a tweed overcoat and dress slacks. His pipe lay on its side on the counter nearby. He only smoked it inside when no customers were in the store.

"The details are freaking amazing. The Luger comes out of the holster, no way!"

Xander held out another figure to the customer. This one was of a civilian woman, her once-white dress soiled and bloody. "Looks a lot like my cheating ex-wife," Xander said and laughed.

The customer looked at the civilian figure in Xander's hand, then raised the miniature Nazi figure up to Xander. "You got any more like this?"

Xander shook his head. "Not right now." He glanced over at the two teenagers standing near the display of magic tricks. His expression didn't change as he watched one of them quickly slide one of the small packages into his coat pocket. He turned back to the customer in front of him and smiled. "But there's plenty more where that came from. Check back in a few weeks," he said.

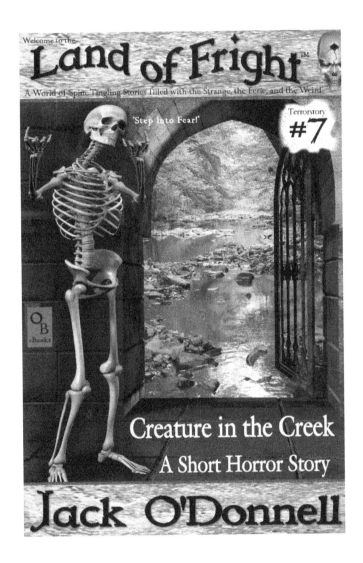

# TERRORSTORY #7
# CREATURE IN THE CREEK

The bright sun and cloudless sky promised a beautiful calm day. They lied. The creature surged up out of the creek only a few feet away from her in an explosive gush of water and clamorous splashing. Carolyn Grace screamed and threw her hands up in front of her, falling backwards off the rock she was squatting on. She couldn't help it. She thought it was a bear about to attack her. It was a dark mass with a darkly colored body and thick, dark arms. A bear was the only thing that made sense in her mind when she first saw it. Because what she saw next made no sense at all.

She sat numbly with her butt buried beneath the

creek's surface as the creek's water slowly moved past her. Carolyn was a twenty year old college student at Duke University. The secluded creek near the house she was staying at was a favorite spot of hers. It was a great place to relax and unwind and just enjoy nature. The water was chilly, but at the moment she didn't feel it at all. Her hands were behind her, her palms flat against the rocky creek floor, holding her up. Her feet were still propped up on the rock she had just been squatting on.

The creature rose up higher and Carolyn immediately saw that it was no bear. She didn't know what it was at all. It had a human shape, with a head, arms and legs, but it was completely covered in leaves and mud and bits of foliage. Was it some demented stalker, some guy dressed up in some kind of camo suit? What did they call it? A ghillie suit. Something snipers used to blend into their surroundings.

"What the fuck, man?" she said. "That was bullshit." So much for a peaceful afternoon away from the books.

The guy in the ghillie suit said nothing.

She suddenly felt the cold water streaming past her and she climbed to her feet. She looked down to see that her shorts were dark with absorbed water. Great, now my money's soaked.

Carolyn stared at the shape. Where was its face? It was about seven feet tall. It stood on the other side of the ragged row of rocks that spanned the thirty-foot width of the creek. She didn't feel safe, but at least the row of rocks that traversed the creek between them gave her a feeling of separation from the guy. Where did he come from? The creek wasn't even that deep. How did he get so close to me without me seeing him? Jesus, he was good. Scary good. The prickles on the back of her neck tingled. "You gonna say something?"

The guy in the ghillie suit said nothing.

"Okay, then." Carolyn moved towards the creek's edge.

The shape followed her, moving parallel to her on the other side of the row of rocks.

"I will kick your ass, motherfucker," Carolyn warned.

And then she saw something on the shape, something that made her blood run cold. Dangling amidst the ragged patches of leaves and mud and twigs, she saw a glistening glint of metal. A silver flash. She froze and stared at the object caught in the ghillie suit.

It was Jerry's medallion. His soccer medallion. No, that can't be. How is that possible?

Carolyn looked closer at the ghillie suit and saw more objects entangled within the muck. There was a rose-shaped pendant. A gold necklace. A charm bracelet. A silver cross. Jesus, was that a tooth? Oh God, it was. It was a gold-filled tooth.

She nervously fingered the pendant dangling between her breasts.

And then she charged for the shore.

She felt something clamp around her wrist, something cold and clammy. She looked down to her left arm to see the guy's fingers wrapped around her wrist. His arms were long enough to reach over the narrow rock barrier that separated them and grab her. She looked up at the faceless mass of debris that masked its face. "I don't think so," she said. She lashed out with a ferocious kick to the guy's midsection.

But when her foot went right through the ghillie suit she knew she wasn't dealing with a man in a camo outfit. She knew she wasn't dealing with a demented stalker. She knew she was dealing with something that wasn't human. Something that wasn't human at all.

The creature tugged sharply at her wrist, pulling her away from the creek's bank. Carolyn stumbled back into the middle of the creek, but kept her balance. Cold water streamed past her ankles.

The creature let go of her arm and suddenly collapsed, dissolving back into the water. Carolyn looked down to see a dark mass maneuvering its way through the rocks, coming over to her side of the rock crossing. Then the creature started to grow again, to take on its humanoid shape as it rose up out of the water right next to her.

Carolyn bolted for the shore, splashing through the shallow water. She expected a cold clammy hand to clamp down on her shoulder at any second, but she made it out of the creek. She moved a few feet inland, then stopped and turned. Something compelled her to look.

The creature was fully formed again, leaves and mud and bits of foliage forming its body. It stood in the creek, just at the water's edge. Watching her.

Carolyn continued backing away from the creek's bank, out of reach of the water, out of reach of the creature's arms. She stared at the creature. The creature stood just inside the creek, staring back.

That's when she saw the creature had eyes. Bright blue eyes buried within the flotsam and jetsam of its face.

Jerry's eyes.
She turned and ran.

---

"Too much hookah," Bonnie said and laughed. Bonnie was a grad student Carolyn had befriended her freshman year and they had become drinking and hookah-smoking buddies. Bonnie had short dark brown hair that contrasted sharply with Carolyn's long blonde hair.

Carolyn looked at her friend. "Bonnie, I kid you not. It stood right there." She pointed to the middle of the creek on the north side of the rocky path that traversed the creek.

"You know how crazy this all sounds, right? It's impossible."

"Am I prone to flights of fancy? Do I ever make shit up?"

Bonnie looked at her. "No. In fact, you don't have much imagination at all."

"Right!" Carolyn looked at her friend. "Hey," she said, a sudden protest in her voice.

Bonnie shrugged. "True that."

Carolyn frowned.

"So, now what?" Bonnie asked. "You gonna wait here for the beastie to come back? Or you gonna check yourself into rehab and take a little break?"

"I did not make this up. I did not imagine it. I swear to God."

"See, you swearing to God don't mean much, now does it?"

"After what I saw here, yes it does. It means a helluva lot right about now."

"Come on, let's go get a glass of wine," Bonnie said. "You are way too wired up for me. You need to chill."

"I saw it, Bonnie."

"That's just not possible, Carolyn. You know that."

Carolyn looked up at her friend. "I know that. I know." She raised her hands up. Her fingers trembled. "Why the fuck do you think my hands are still trembling?"

Bonnie reached out and took Carolyn's hands into hers. "You were supposed to wait until I get my masters in psych before going off the deep end." Bonnie smiled playfully. "Girl, I look at you and my brain goes *k-ching*! That girl is gonna be money in the bank when I start my practice."

"I wish I could laugh at that, but right now I can't." Tears welled up in her eyes, but Carolyn refused to let them fall. "Jesus, Bonnie. I'm scared."

Bonnie pulled her close, hugging her tight. "Shh, it's all right. Jerry—" she paused. "That — that was rough. I know. It takes a lot longer to get over something like that than people think."

<hr>

Carolyn looked through the binoculars. She could barely make out the creek through the tangle of trees and brush, but she could see part of the rocky outcropping that crossed the body of water. The water flowed at its usual pace. A squirrel darted across the rocks. A bird landed on one of the stones, but then quickly flew off. Nothing big stirred. The creature in the creek was nowhere to be seen.

She lowered the binoculars. Was Bonnie right? Did I just imagine it? No. There's no way I just imagined that. I saw that thing standing in the middle of the creek. That fucking thing grabbed my arm.

She felt guilty for missing biology class, but she just couldn't concentrate on any of her school work right now. She moved closer and put the binoculars to her eyes. She kept thinking of Jerry and those blue eyes the creature had. They were Jerry's eyes. She was sure of it.

Carolyn stood on the bridge. Suicide Bridge. That's what everyone called it. They tried putting up fences and barriers, but none of that really helped prevent anything. The determined ones always found a way over them. Nothing was going to stop them from making the leap of death if that's what they wanted to do. They hadn't stopped Jerry.

She thought about the soccer medallion she had seen on the creature. Is that what drove Jerry over the edge? Because his shitty grades knocked him off the team? He didn't even leave a note. He just quit. Quit on the world. Quit on school. Quit on her.

Carolyn looked at the river's water far below. How many others had jumped from here? Half a dozen? Scores? She didn't know. But she knew it was enough to give the nickname strength. A chill wind blew past and she hugged her arms to her chest. Just standing on the bridge gave her the willies. How many people stood in the exact spot she was standing in and breathed their last breaths?

She moved along the bridge, not wanting to stand

still in any one spot for too long. She lifted her gaze, following the flow of the water, moving her gaze along the river's path. She knew where the river ultimately let out. She knew where it ended.

At the creek. Her creek. Her favorite spot in the whole world was like the end of a sewer drain for tormented souls. God, that's a disgusting thing to think. A sewer for lost souls.

❦

Carolyn moved closer back to the creek each day. Now she was close enough to clearly see it without the binoculars. The newspaper had just printed a story about another suicide. A mother of three children who just lost her family in a car accident. The mother had been the driver. It was almost something Carolyn could understand. Almost. She still wouldn't have done it. She would've fought even harder to survive, to keep their memories alive.

She looked at the creek. Was she in there now? Was that woman in the waters? Was her tormented soul floating in the current?

❦

Carolyn sat on a log near the water's edge. She absently tossed a pebble into the creek. The tiny rock made a mute splashing sound. The sky was still clear above the creek, but a bank of grey clouds was visible in the distance. The slight wind slowly brought them closer.

Nothing. It had been weeks now and she had seen no sight of the creature. The memory of it had started to fade. She could almost convince herself that it had just been a weird dream. A terrifyingly weird dream.

She stood up and move to the bank. She stood right at the edge of the creek. The water glistened and shimmered as it moved through the tumbled mass of rocks that traversed the creek's width. She raised her foot and moved it out over the creek, contemplating stepping on the first rock. She pulled her foot back.

That's when the creature rose up out of the creek right in front of her. She didn't scream. She didn't run. She just watched it rise up out of the water a mere few feet away. It still had the same shape, a mass of leaves and mud and foliage in human form. She immediately spotted Jerry's medallion lodged in its body. She saw something else she didn't remember seeing before. It was like a tattoo on the creature's left arm, like a shape had been stamped into one of the leaves that made up the creature's inhuman body. She remembered the picture of the woman who had lost her children in the car accident. She had a tattoo on her arm. A tattoo of a butterfly. It was the same tattoo she now saw on the creature.

Carolyn looked up at the creature's eyes. They weren't Jerry's eyes anymore. Now they were brown, dull and flat. Were those the woman's eyes? Was she in there with Jerry now? Was she part of the creature now?

Then the eyes changed as she stared at them. They flashed to a bright blue. Then they changed to a hazel, then back to the dull brown. Then back to the blue.

"Jerry?"

The eyes remained a bright blue. The creature stared at her mutely. A sadness filled its blue eyes, but it was a different kind of sadness than Carolyn's. Hers was an angry sadness, a bitter sadness. The creature's sadness was laced with pity, poisoned with its own self-absorbed sorrow. The creature cocked its head, ever so slightly, but the movement was there. The creature raised its arm and pointed upstream.

She knew where he was pointing. It wasn't towards the row of trees that lined the creek. It wasn't towards the road that lay a hundred yards in the distance. It was pointing towards the bridge. Suicide Bridge. She shook her head. "I don't want to go there." A shiny shimmering wetness coated her eyes. She refused to let the tears fall. She clenched her teeth tight.

The creature's pointing finger remained rigidly in place.

"No, Jerry, don't ask me to do that." She missed him terribly. They had such good times together. Going to movies. Going out dancing. Hiking together. Riding their bikes for miles. Just sitting around talking and laughing at their own stupid jokes. She didn't understand why he had left her. She just didn't understand. Did the bridge hold the answers? Not the bridge, but what came after. Did that hold the answers?

The creature's finger thrust forward, an obviously insistent gesture.

Carolyn looked at the creature, then in the direction it was pointing. She stared at the creek; she could hear the water babbling, making soft whispering sounds as it moved through the rocks. She realized what she needed to do. "I don't want to go there alone," she finally said. "Come with me." She pointed to the creek. "You don't belong there anymore." She looked at the creature. "You belong with me." She curled her fingers inwards, repeating the motion a few times. "Come."

The creature stood motionless in the creek. The water flowed past its legs, ruffling the leaves and debris that made up its feet.

She curled her fingers again. "Come on, Jerry. Come with me. Please. I want you to be with me." She stood straighter, forcing away all the sadness, pushing out a smile onto her lips.

The creature took a hesitant step forward, then another.

Carolyn smiled brightly. "That's it. That's it."

The creature took another step. Then another. The creature reached the bank of the creek and stopped. It glanced down at the edge, at the dry land just beyond the flowing water, then up to Carolyn's face.

She took a few steps up the path, moving away from the creek. She looked over her shoulder, motioning for the creature to follow. "Come on, we'll go up to the house first and just talk. Like old times. Then you can take me to the bridge."

The creature did not move.

Carolyn stopped and turned back around to face the creature. She took a few steps back towards the creek. "Jerry, don't make me go there alone. Don't do that. You know how much I hate being alone." She smiled. "Now come on. Time to go."

The creature raised a foot and hesitantly touched it to the creek's bank.

"See," Carolyn said. "You can do this. Come on."

The creature put its weight on its forward foot and rose up out of the creek, bringing its second foot out of the creek. Water dripped off its muddy, leaf-coated foot as it brought its leg forward to lower its foot onto the bank.

"Piece of cake, right?" Carolyn smiled.

The creature now stood completely out of the water.

"Come on." She turned and headed up the path.

The creature followed, taking one hesitant, shuffling step after the other.

They moved past a fallen log, past a smattering of twigs and branches. They brushed by plants and low grass; Carolyn was very conscious of staying several yards in front of the creature, keeping out of its reach as they moved.

They were about halfway up the path when she noticed the creature was slowing. Each step seemed more difficult, more labored for the creature. It stumbled once and nearly fell. She continued moving. Then the creature stumbled again and fell to its knees.

It never got back up.

Carolyn moved back to it and stood watching as the leaves started to fall off the creature. It was withering, drying up from being away from its life-giving water. She said nothing. She just watched. She was morbidly fascinated at what lay beneath the creature's outer shell of leaves and mud and debris. But she soon realized it was no shell. It was like skin, skin that was starting to flake and peel. There was nothing hidden beneath it, just more leaves, more mud, more debris.

But the eyes. What about the eyes? Where did those come from?

The creature reached up a hand towards her, its fingers groping, grasping for her. She did not reach out to it.

Then the hand fell, collapsing into a formless lump of leaves and twigs.

The arm soon followed. Soon, all that remained was the creature's torso and its head. None shall pass. Carolyn thought of the black knight in Monty Python and the Holy Grail and nearly laughed aloud but she bit back the madness.

She looked at the creature's head, its face. The eyes were still there. Beseeching. Pleading for something. "You don't belong here," she said. "You don't belong in this world anymore." The corners of her eyes glistened. "You don't belong with me," she said, finally releasing the words she so wanted to say. "You gave up on me. I'm not giving up on myself."

And then the creature's head dissolved, leaving nothing but a jumbled mass of leaves and mud and creek debris with a vague resemblance to arms, legs, and fingers. Carolyn moved to the mass and stood over it. She saw the rose-shaped pendant amidst the debris, and the silver cross. She knew Jerry's soccer medallion was in the pile somewhere, but she couldn't bring herself to stick her hand into the muck. Nothing moved. Whatever unholy power had brought the monstrosity to life was gone. The creature was dead. She looked down at the ground to see two blue colored stones amidst the debris. Stones. They were just stones. Jerry was gone. He had finally let go of this world. Had she done the right thing? Was it right for her to decide Jerry's fate? She didn't know. She just knew it wasn't right for his soul to be stuck in that godforsaken jumble of mud and muck.

And finally the tears fell, falling in streams down her cheeks, drawing a wet path down her face. They rolled over the corners of her mouth, down her chin, and dropped away from her. Her tears hit the mass of leaves and mud and brush that lay in a lump on the dry path at her feet.

The mass shifted, but so slightly that she didn't notice it behind the blurry veil of her tears.

Carolyn turned and walked away, fighting back the sobs that threatened to overwhelm her. She picked up her pace and started to run, her tears streaming down her face.

Behind her, on the path, the creature's finger twitched.

The dark clouds above threatened rain.

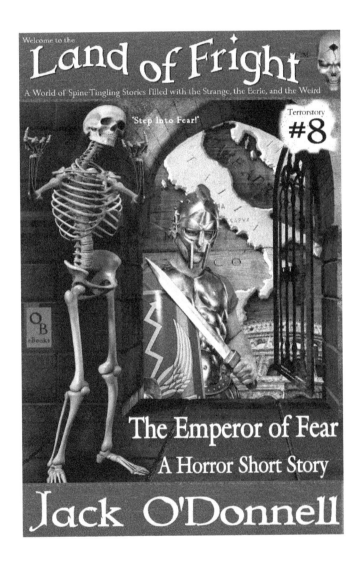

## TERRORSTORY #8
## THE EMPEROR OF FEAR

There were no letters on the wooden crate. No descriptions. Nothing to indicate what was inside. Aurelius circled the crate, running his hand along the smooth wood. He was a thin man with thinning brown hair. He wore a white tunic tied at the waist with a black cord. The tunic had seen a lot of wear over the years, as had the man. They were both wrinkled and weathered by time.

Aurelius stood inside the hypogeum, the vast network of tunnels and passages that ran under the coliseum that Domitian had added when he became emperor of Rome. He tried to peer inside the crate, but the slats were too narrow and it was just too dark in this section of the tunnels to make anything out. There was certainly no elephant inside; the crate was far too small for that. No inscription indicating a tiger. No lion.

An unfamiliar trilling sound came from within the crate. It was a sound unlike anything Aurelius had ever heard. He had worked with quite a lot of exotic animals over the last few years at the Flavium Amphitheater, but the sound this one made was not recognizable. It had a bird-like quality to it, but he knew there was no bird inside the crate.

"What is it?" Caracas asked.

Aurelius shook his head.

His friend stopped at his side and stared at the crate along with him. Caracas was a burly man with a bald head and a pug nose. "Who brought it in here?"

Aurelius shrugged. "No markings. No sigil. No crest. I don't know."

"Is it for tomorrow's games?"

"I can only assume so," Aurelius said.

"Maybe this is for Carpo? He's the best bestiaries in this place."

"Maybe. He doesn't like to be surprised by the animal he's fighting, though. Remember when they sprang that rhinoceros on him?"

Caracas nodded. "That was not a good day." He circled the crate. "You going to open it?"

"Yes." Aurelius did not move.

Caracas waited for a moment. "I mean now."

"Fetch me a pry bar." Aurelius pointed down the tunnel, leaving his hand outstretched.

Caracas turned and trotted back down the tunnel.

Aurelius circled the crate again. The sound came again, but this time it was not a trilling sound. It sounded like weeping. Like a child weeping. He felt a chill engulf his body. It sounded like Marcinia just before she died. It sounded just like the girl he had killed in the streets. *I didn't kill her; it was an accident. She ran out right in front of the horses. But you weren't watching the road, were you? You were too busy getting pleasured by that Thracian whore, weren't you? It wasn't my fault!*

The weeping sound grew louder.

By the gods, was there really a child in there? "Hello," he called out. Aurelius put his face closer to the wood slats. "Is there someone in there?"

The weeping sound stopped.

Caracas returned with a pry bar and handed it to Aurelius. Aurelius put an edge of the pry bar to the lid, but his hand was shaking so badly he couldn't fit the end of the bar into the crack of space between the lid and the body of the crate.

"Something wrong?" Caracas asked.

"I thought I heard something in there."

"Heard what? An animal?"

"No. I don't know." *A girl. A girl I killed.* "Something." Finally, Aurelius managed to slide the pry bar in place and gave it a tug upwards. The wood cracked and the lid started to lift away.

"Stop! By the gods, stop! Stop!"

Aurelius and Caracas turned to see a man striding towards them. He wore a full toga atop his tunic. A purple stripe adorned the toga. Aurelius didn't recognize the man, but he was clearly a man of stature by the nature of his dress. Most likely a new senator. Everyone else would have had enough sense not to wear a cumbersome toga in the hot tunnels beneath the sands of the arena. Several men in plain tunics followed the senator.

"Are you touched with fever?" the senator exclaimed. "Do you know what's in there?"

"No, can't say that I do," Aurelius replied. "That's why we were going to open it."

"Well I do. And it needs to stay in there."

Aurelius squinted at the man in the purple-striped toga. "Who are you?" he asked.

The man looked down his nose at Aurelius with a sour expression. "I am Senator Egnatius. Favored son of Rome."

"What is it?" Caracas asked.

Senator Egnatius look at the crate. He reached out with his hand but stopped before he touched the wooden container. He turned a solemn face to Aurelius and Caracas. "It's justice. Justice for my son."

"I have to see what's in there," Aurelius said.

Caracas took a bite from his bread. "Just wait. You'll see it tomorrow."

Aurelius drummed his fingers on the wooden table. "I don't think I can wait." The plate of stuffed olives sat untouched before him.

Caracas frowned at him.

"You didn't hear it. I did. It sounded like a child. Like a crying child."

"He said it was justice for his son."

"What does that even mean? Is his son in that crate? Is that who was crying?" Aurelius shook his head. "No one has ever brought a person in here inside a sealed up crate. Never. Not even the worst of the criminals. And I've been here since Titus first opened it up." Aurelius looked at his friend. "Animals, yes. People, no."

"We'll find out tomorrow. It's probably just some weird beast somebody found in Africa." Caracas broke off another chunk of bread. He waved it at Aurelius. "Remember those stories about when Julius Caesar brought the first giraffe to Rome? My father used to tell me stories about it. No one could believe such an animal could exist. Yet, it did. And now we take them for granted. Same thing with whatever animal is in that crate. It'll be strange at first, but then we'll take it for granted." He popped the bread into his mouth.

Aurelius drummed his fingers on the table.

There was no waiting until tomorrow. Aurelius set the pry bar down and eased the lid of the crate to the side, moving it just enough so he could peer inside. He raised the oil lamp he held in his hand and the wan light from the flame flowed into the crate.

She sat huddled in the corner, her knees pulled up to her chest. Her white tunic was streaked with dried mud and dried blood. Her head hung down, her long black hair shielding her face from the yellow light cast by the lamp.

Aurelius opened his mouth to speak, but no words came out. This was not possible. He had paid for her funeral. He had seen her buried. Yet here Marcinia sat, huddled and filthy in a crate.

She slowly lifted her head to look up at him. Her blue eyes were filled with something he had never seen in someone so young before. The rage he felt emanating from her buffeted him like a gale wind and he staggered back away from the crate. He had been working beneath the sands of the arena for years, dealing with savage animals from all over the empire, with savage men convicted of the most heinous, hate-filled crimes, but he had never seen the intensity of a look like that.

"Help me," she said. The words came out in a demanding tone.

Aurelius stood still for a long moment in the dark tunnel. The oil lamp was down at his side now, the light illuminating his narrow face in long shadows.

"Help me, Aurelius."

The sound of his name was like a physical blow; it felt like a hand had clutched at his heart. Aurelius took several steps away from the crate, backing up until he struck the stone wall of the corridor. He heard sounds coming from within the crate, shuffling sounds, more movement. He raised the oil lamp higher, throwing the light on the narrow opening he had made when he slid the lid aside.

A hand appeared. Small fingers curled around the edge of the wooden crate. Another small hand appeared, this one pushing the lid away, making the opening wider.

*By the gods. She's coming out. She's coming out!*

Then her face appeared, popping abruptly out of the opening.

Aurelius started and nearly lost his hold on the lamp. It took all his will not to urinate on himself.

Her face was a misshapen mess. Her left cheek was flattened to the width of the wax tablet his son used to write on at school. Her forehead had several deep, dried gashes cut into it. Her mouth was twisted into a weird grimace that made it look like she was smiling and frowning all at the same time. "Aren't you going to help me out?" she asked.

Her mouth moved and he understood the words, but Aurelius found it hard to believe such a grotesque set of lips could make any coherent sounds at all. He didn't answer. His mouth had no moisture and he struggled to form words.

Marcinia climbed out of the crate to stand before him on crooked legs. Her right knee and right shin were shattered and shriveled, making her right leg shorter than her left leg, giving her an off balance appearance. "Like what you see?" she asked.

Aurelius shook his head. "What—?" The sound of his own voice startled him and he stopped. He licked his dry lips with a dry tongue.

"I like what I see," she said. "I see it all over you. I can see it shining all over your body." She made a grotesque sniffing noise. "I can smell it, too." She took a step closer.

Aurelius tried to back up through the stone wall behind him, but there was nowhere for him to go.

"Ahh, it's getting stronger," Marcinia said. A black swollen tongue slid out of her mouth and ran over her distorted lips.

"What — do you — want?"

She shook her head. "Aurelius, you know what I want."

"What — are you?"

"You know what I am."

Aurelius shook his head. "No. I — I don't know what you are."

She cocked her head. "I am what I want."

Aurelius could only stare at her.

"Justice."

Aurelius didn't have time to scream before she set upon him.

After Justice was served, she cleaned up the area, kicking sand over the red stains near the crate as best she could with her deformed legs. She climbed back up inside the crate and pulled the lid securely back down into place.

Caracas dipped his bread into a pool of olive oil on a plate before him and took a bite. Behind him, gladiators moved about, some fully dressed in their battle gear, others preparing for their afternoon fights, others just arriving. Other gladiators were in their holding rooms, awaiting the call to the arena that would come in a few hours. Above them, the arena was loud and raucous. It was still the early morning, so the animal hunts were still going on. "Where in Pluto's ass is Aurelius?" Caracas grumbled.

"Don't know," another man answered. He was Gratius, a thin man with short brown hair. A scar was seared across his skull from just above his left eye to the back of his head.

Caracas glanced at the sealed crate that was positioned near ramp thirteen, then looked back to Gratius. "He was dying to see what was inside that crate."

"He's probably with that Thracian whore again. That's where I'd be if I was him. She's a real beauty, that one is."

Caracas nodded. He took a sip of warm wine from his mug.

A third man joined them, sitting down at the table. He pointed to the crate. "So what's in there?" He was Talaver, a tall man with a smooth face and curly black hair.

"Don't know. I think they are saving it for the executions. Talk is the emperor is in attendance today. He's going to stay through the executions just to see it."

"Domitian is here today?" Gratius's fingers shook. "I hate when he attends."

"Gratius! You had best curb your tongue before it gets cut out." Caracas's words came out curt and sharp.

"It puts everyone on edge," Gratius said. "It ruins the show. Everyone's afraid of him."

"He is your emperor. You *should* fear him," Caracas said.

Gratius stood and walked away.

"What's that about?" Talaver asked.

Caracas watched Gratius walk away and then turned to Talaver. "The emperor pulled his son out of the crowd and made him fight in the games. His son didn't live to see the night. Two lions ripped him to shreds."

Talaver took a deep drink from his mug.

Many of the first tier seats in the podium level were usually empty by this time of the day. It was the noon hour and many of the higher class citizens had no stomach for the brutality of the mid-day executions. But not today. Today the podium level was full. The senators were in strong attendance, all of them dressed in their full toga regalia with the distinctive purple borders.

The second and third tiers of seats were also brimming with male citizens, all dressed in their formal heavy white woolen togas and sandals. Women filled the fourth tier of steep wooden seats that were set up in the gallery running around the very top wall of the coliseum. Some of the poorer male citizens dressed in drab grey cloth sat amongst the women. There were no standing room positions left unfilled. The amphitheater was filled with excited, expectant Romans.

The emperor remained in his seat in the Imperial Box. Domitian was dressed in his purple toga, a laurel leaf crown encircling his head. He knew several of the senators criticized him behind his back for remaining during the executions, but he rebuffed such idle talk. He felt it was important to see that justice was done to the ill-begotten dregs of his empire. He didn't always stay for the executions, but today he was in attendance and he had no intention of leaving. Egnatius had promised him a special surprise.

The sand on the arena floor was stained with the blood of dead criminals. A lion had been set loose on two women, convicted thieves, and the animal had made quick kills of them. Five other men had been given daggers and they had fought to the death. The winner's victory only lasted a few seconds as he was summarily executed with a quick slice across his throat.

One man now stood alone in the sand. He was dressed in nothing but a tattered loincloth. His black curly hair was matted with dirt and grime. His flesh was pale, his skin soft and unweathered. Clearly not a man of hard outdoor labor. He was a criminal convicted of murder, now awaiting his time to die.

Senator Egnatius rose from his honored seated position near the emperor and addressed the crowd. His voice was strong, carrying across the arena to the fellow men of stature on the lower levels opposite them, and up into the wooden seats far above where the common men and the women sat. "My friends of Rome, today our magnificent emperor brings you a creature never before seen in this arena. A creature never before seen in any arena in our great empire. A creature from the deep jungles of Africa where only savages and the brave hunters of Rome dare to enter."

The gathered throng in the middle and upper seats clapped and cheered. The people of Rome loved surprises. Domitian smiled. Even the senators made exuberant noises.

A ramp opened up on the arena floor and the crate rose up out of the ground, moving up out of the darkness beneath the sands into the bright sunlight that bathed the arena in its golden glow.

Egnatius held up his hand, waiting for the audience to become quiet again. He pointed to the pale man standing in the sand. "The vile wretch who now cowers in the arena will be the creature's first victim. This thing who calls himself a man betrayed my son and murdered him in his sleep by stabbing him in the back." The pale man was his son's scorned lover, but Egnatius felt no need to mention that detail.

Egnatius motioned to several workers waiting in

the wings on the arena floor below. The men moved to the crate and pried open the lid, sliding it fully off the crate. The workers took the top with them and they disappeared down the ramp, vanishing beneath the arena. The ramp closed, moving back up into place.

"Now he will face the beast called Justice!" Senator Egnatius proclaimed.

As if on cue, the four sides of the crate fell, each one falling away from the center at the same time, revealing the beast within.

Silence blanketed the coliseum. Then shrill, raucous laughter exploded out from the crowd. Fingers pointed and the laughter grew louder and louder.

A shriveled old woman stood in the center of the crate. She was naked, her sagging breasts nearly touching her belly button as she hunched over. Her skin was thick with wrinkles. The pale criminal cowered before the old woman, fear clearly gripping him at the sight of her.

The emperor turned a disappointed gaze to Egnatius. "This is the justice you bring to your son's murderer? Some sick old woman?"

Egnatius stared open-mouthed at the scene on the arena floor below.

"Answer me, Egnatius." The emperor's face was stern. Everyone who was standing near the emperor took a few steps back away from him.

Egnatius turned to the emperor. "That is not the creature I saw. That is not the beast that was captured in the jungle."

Laughter continued to fill the arena.

The emperor's face darkened. "You shame me,

Egnatius."

"No, that is not what I saw! That is not the animal that was in the crate." Egnatius looked at Emperor Domitian with terror in his eyes. "I swear it."

The naked old woman limped toward the pale man. Sniggering sounds of chortling and guffawing continued to fill the arena.

The emperor's face darkened even further. "You shame me in front of all of Rome!"

"No," Egnatius said, but the sound was merely a whimper.

The emperor made a motion with his hand and Egnatius suddenly found himself hurtling through the air. He hit the sandy floor of the arena hard; sand splashed up into his mouth. He rose shakily to his feet, trying to maintain his dignity with lips caked with sand. He looked up at the emperor. "I beg you, do not do this." The words came out garbled and he had no choice but to turn his head aside and spit out the wet grains from his mouth.

"I only do as your speech proclaimed," the emperor said. "Justice will be served."

Suddenly the pale criminal was on Egnatius, punching and kicking at him. Egnatius did his best to fend him off, but he was no match for the deranged fury of the man. The surprise of the attack caught Egnatius completely off guard. The pale man knocked him to the ground and leaped on top of him. Egnatius had no chance to retaliate. He was face down in the sand, the man's knees pinning his back to the arena floor. The pale man put his hands around Egnatius's neck and held a tight grip around his throat. The pale man squeezed and squeezed. Finally, Egnatius was still, dead on the arena floor. Breathing hard, the pale man clambered off the lifeless senator and rose shakily to his feet.

The crowd cheered.

"Look!" someone shouted.

"Where is the old woman?"

"She's gone."

"Who is that?"

Questions and exclamatory shouts rang out all around the arena. A collective gasp erupted from the crowd like a blustery wind whistling through a field of wheat.

The emperor jumped to his feet and move to the edge of the platform, gazing at the creature with a clenched jaw. "What is the meaning of this?"

No one answered.

Emperor Domitian could only stare in disbelief at the creature standing in the middle of the crate, could only gape in growing terror at the beast who now looked exactly like himself.

⚜

"My fellow Romans!" the creature-emperor shouted. It raised its arms up, beseeching the crowd to listen.

The crowd stayed quiet. Domitian could only watch silent in rapt fascination at this doppelgänger of himself.

"There are those among you who have been led down a fool's path." The creature-emperor turned as he spoke, shouting to all who sat around the arena. "There are those among you who believe in a false god." The creature-emperor finished his turn and stared at the emperor's box. "There are those among

134

you who will pay for your misguided devotion."

"Kill him!" Domitian raged, finally getting hold of his senses and pushing the shock and disbelief away. He raised a trembling hand and thrust his finger at the creature-emperor. "Kill him!"

The armed soldiers near Domitian did not move.

"Kill him!" Domitian shrieked. His lips trembled.

The soldiers glanced at each other. Some of them drew their blades. But none of them made a move towards the creature-emperor. They kept looking at the emperor before them and then back to the creature-emperor standing in the sands just below.

"My fellow Romans!" the creature-emperor called out. "I am the one who decides who lives or dies." The creature-emperor raised its hand and pointed a steady finger at the emperor standing on the platform in the Imperial Box. "Today, he dies. Toss him to the sands."

Many senators turned to stare at the man dressed in purple standing near them. In their eyes, the man suddenly looked feeble and pathetic with his trembling lips and shaking fingers. This weak man was no emperor. He was an impostor. They set upon him, climbing into the Imperial Box to attack him. The madness quickly spread and others in the crowd followed, ripping, tearing, clawing, biting. Domitian barely had time to utter a pleading cry for his life. Within moments, it was over. Domitian was dead, his torn and tattered body covered with blood, his purple toga drenched in dark stains. They picked up his body and tossed it to the sands. The laurel leaf crown splashed up a tiny puff of sand as it hit the arena floor.

The new emperor put his foot on the purple-clothed corpse that lay on the ground before him and threw his hands up in the air triumphantly. "Rome, the false god is dead!"

The crowd was silent. No one could seem to comprehend what was happening before their very eyes. It had all happened so fast. It was all so unbelievable.

The pale man moved over to the new emperor and stood next to him. He dropped to one knee and bowed before the new emperor, holding the laurel leaf crown in his hand.

"There are those among you who love me," the new emperor declared. Some in the crowd cheered, but it was a very unenthusiastic cheer. The new emperor patted the pale man affectionately on the head. He took the offered crown and placed the laurel leaf atop his head. He looked up at the senators in the first tier. "There are those among you who hate me." His gaze moved up the tiers, up the rows of seats. "But you will all fear me."

Some in the crowd dared to boo the proclamation.

The new emperor immediately honed in on one of the dissenting voices. He raised his hand and pointed to a senator in the front row. "That man. Throw him to the sands."

Several armored soldiers wielding swords moved to the offending senator, grabbed him, and hurled him to the sand.

The crowd erupted into cheers and applause as another man in a purple-striped toga fell dead to the arena floor. The coliseum sands were now littered with the bodies of half a dozen dead senators and a few corpses in white woolen togas. No more dissenting voices were heard from the crowd.

The new emperor again raised his arms in triumph. "I have given you a games for the ages! You will tell your children, and they will tell their children, and they will tell their children!"

The crowd erupted into cheers and applause.

The new emperor liked this new land he found himself in. He decided he would stay. There was a great need for justice here. He smelled fear all around him and the smell was delicious.

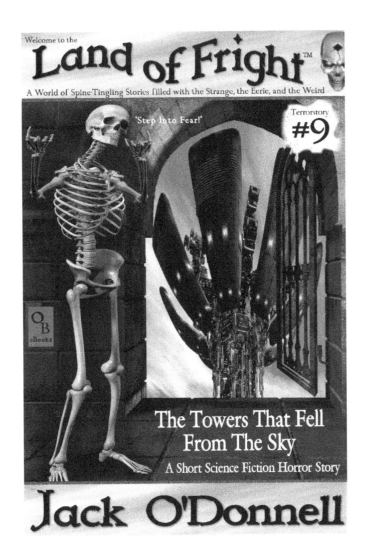

# TERRORSTORY #9
# THE TOWERS THAT
# FELL FROM THE SKY

**T**hey landed on **Tuesday**.

They were huge towering structures, most of them reaching hundreds of feet into the sky, some of them reaching thousands of feet. Some were squat, some were long and tall. All of them were massive. Their shiny metallic surfaces glittered brightly in the hot sunlight of Egypt, shimmered in the moonlight near Stonehenge, sparkled in the rain in Singapore, gleamed near the rim of the Grand Canyon.

They had come seemingly from nowhere. Radar had not picked them up. A few scattered telescopic reports had come in of weird objects in the sky, but nothing substantial, nothing anyone could really react to. It all happened too fast. The towering structures just came thundering down out of the sky, landing with heavy thuds that shook the ground for miles around.

They landed in Chicago. They landed in Paris. They landed in New York. Hundreds of cities across the globe felt their arrivals.

The world panicked on Wednesday.

Jeremy Rann studied the images of several of the alien structures on his tablet. "Did you see the one that landed in Quebec?" he asked the woman sitting next to him.

Bianca Green nodded without looking up from her tablet. She was in her mid-fifties, an attractive woman who refused to let herself go gracefully gray. Her black hair was elegantly tinted with just a hint of red. "It's similar to the one that landed in Iceland."

"You see any points of entry?"

"Not sure." She circled an area on the image with her finger and swiped at it, electronically throwing the picture on Jeremy's screen. "But look at that. Don't those look like indentations? Possibly some kind of door?"

Jeremy looked at the image that slid onto his screen. He was in his mid-twenties, under Bianca's expert tutelage. He still lived at home with his single mother, having only just graduated from Greenlore Online University. His friend teased him about Bianca, telling Jeremy he went straight from one mother figure in his life to another. He shrugged that off. He liked Bianca. She was a good mentor. He studied the very slight discoloration that Bianca had circled on the image. It could very well be some kind of door. The lines were very thin and barely discernible, but they were definitely there. It was a small square. It could be some kind of door panel.

"There are some up at the top, some in the middle, and some at the bottom. If I was going to put in a weapons system, that's where I would put my weaponry. Something to hit high altitude traffic, middle air traffic, and ground traffic," Bianca said.

Jeremy nodded. Bianca was wearing the blue button up blouse that he really liked. She always left the top two buttons unbuttoned. Jeremy was convinced she did that just to tease him. It was downright odd how many times she dropped things on the floor and had to bend over to pick them up. Was he really not supposed to try and sneak a peek at her breasts? She had a very nice chest. But she hadn't dropped anything lately, and he didn't expect she would. Not today.

"It looks like they encircle the entire structure, so they are covering a three hundred sixty degree angle of attack. All of the other structures have similar markings," Bianca said.

"Any messages yet?" Jeremy asked. "They giving off any kind of signals?"

Bianca nodded. "We are getting some weird signal, but nobody's deciphered it yet. Chuck is trying. He thinks it's some kind of language because of the few patterns he's seeing. His whole team is on it. He's in communication with about a dozen other teams across the globe, too. The moment somebody translates it, we'll know."

Jeremy looked back at his screen, staring at the massive towers. "What the hell are they?

"Tell us what you see, Lisa Anne." Roger Cransfeld held his finger over his ear, pressing his ear-piece tighter against his head. He was sitting at his anchor desk at the LFN headquarters in Chicago. He was an African American in his mid-thirties, a handsome man with a strong, deep voice. He looked back up at the camera. "We've lost visual with Lisa Anne in the field, but we still have audio. Please bear with us." He looked sideways towards his ear. "Go on, Lisa Anne."

"Something's definitely happening. The tower on Lake Shore Drive is making noises. Very loud noises. They are humming and clicking."

Screams could be heard coming over the audio.

"What's happening?" Roger asked. "We hear screaming."

"My God, they're gun barrels! Dozens of slots are opening in the tower and gun barrels are coming out! Some of them are gigantic."

More screams played out over the audio.

Roger pressed his fingers to his ear. "What's happening, Lisa Anne?"

"They're aiming in every direction. It's not dozens. It's hundreds, Roger. Hundreds."

Roger dropped his hand from his ear. He sat quietly for a long moment, saying nothing. He stared down at his news desk. Then, he popped the ear-piece out of his ear and dropped it to the desk. He casually unhooked the microphone attached to his shirt and dropped that to the desk. He paused for a moment, then picked the tiny microphone back up. He looked at the camera. "I'm going home to be with my wife and kids. Good luck, everyone."

He dropped the microphone back to the desk, stood up, and walked out of the camera's range.

"You getting this?" Jeremy asked Bianca.

Bianca nodded. "They are starting to glow. It's real faint, but it's definitely there."

"Like they are powering up."

Bianca nodded. "The readings are starting to climb. There is a lot of energy starting to accumulate in those towers. A helluva lot of energy."

Jeremy picked up his smartphone from the desktop. "I'd better call my mom. She's on a cruise in the Caribbean." He hit his mother's contact icon and waited. There was no signal. He looked at Bianca. "No signal."

Bianca nodded softly.

Jeremy quickly tapped a text message and sent it. "Maybe she'll get that." He set his phone down and looked at Bianca for a long moment. He wanted to see the wrinkles at the corners of her eyes turn up. They always did that when she smiled. He had an intense need to see her smile right now. "Hey, Bianca," he said.

She looked over at him. Their gazes met and held. He reached out his hand to her, but she didn't take it.

"I —" he began, but she didn't let him finish.

"Don't say anything, Jeremy," she said to him. She

glanced around the room, then looked back to him. "We've got work to do right now."

He pulled his hand back. Right now, she said. He held out the hope that later was still in the mix.

Stores were looted with wild abandon. Glass and debris littered nearly every street in every small town in America. Fires burned. Sirens wailed but no one answered their desperate cries. There wasn't a cop to be seen anywhere. The National Guard was already fully deployed to the areas around the massive towers, but even many of them had simply gone home to be with their families.

Neighbors begged to be let into bunkers. Smug survivalists turned them away.

Many families huddled around television screens. There was nowhere to hide; there was nowhere else to go. They watched the news and waited.

"Any news from Chuck and his team?" Jeremy asked. He stood next to Bianca, holding two covered cups in his hand.

Bianca shook her head. "Nothing yet. A few false leads, but nothing concrete." She glanced up at him. "Any word from your mother?"

Jeremy shook his head. "No. Nothing seems to be getting through." He stretched a cup out towards her. "I brought you some coffee. Half decaf with French vanilla, right?"

Bianca nodded. She took the offered coffee. "Thanks."

Their fingers briefly touched in the exchange of the cup.

Jeremy sat in his chair next to her.

He glanced down at her hand, then back up to her face, but she was already looking back at her monitor. He watched her take a sip of her coffee. What an absurdly ridiculous time to get an erection. But he urgently, desperately wanted her. The touch of her fingers on his was immensely arousing. The sight of Bianca's lips gently touching the lid of the cup as she took a sip of her coffee was downright erotic. He wanted her right then and there.

But he said nothing. Jeremy turned his attention back to the towers that filled his screen. The towers were definitely powering up. He could see their energy signatures rapidly rising on his monitor.

Several gang members in Chicago stood in front of one of the towers on 44th street. They had gang symbols tattooed on their bare arms. Several of them sported red bandannas. Most of them had guns tucked into their waistbands or behind a belt. They made no attempt to hide their weaponry.

One of the gang members fired off a shot at the tower and the bullet ricocheted wildly off the metal surface of the structure, pinging off a nearby car. Another gang member slapped him on the shoulder. "You hit my car, bitch."

Ricardo Gutierez strutted closer to the tower. What the fuck was this piece of shit thing doing in the middle of his street? Nobody could get by it without driving through people's lawns. Through his lawn. He just mowed the fucking thing, too. He stopped when he was within a few feet of the towering structure. The metal glowed very faintly and it gave off a slight crackling noise. Ricardo raised his hand and reached out towards the metal surface.

"Don't touch it, man," someone shouted at him.

Ricardo touched the tips of his fingers to the tower and was instantly electrocuted. His body glowed bright for a red hot second and then he crumbled down to the ground in a heap. He stared blankly at the tower through glassy eyes. A faint plume of smoke rose up out of his mouth.

Everyone nearby scurried away from the tower.

Bianca leaned over Jeremy, pointing to a small area on one of the towers that filled his monitor. "They look like some kind of solar panels, don't they?" she asked.

He could feel her breasts on his back. There was no way that was accidental, he thought. Is that her nipple? My God. The bulge in his pants ached to be let out. Did she just ask him something? "What?" he muttered.

She leaned in closer, pressing herself even tighter against him. "Right there. That looks like a solar panel. I think they might be absorbing energy from the sun."

Jeremy concentrated on the area she was pointing to. She was right. They did look like solar panels. "And powering up their weapons," he added.

She pulled away from him and he immediately missed the feel of her body, the warmth of her closeness.

❦

The Pentagon buzzed with incessant activity. Hundreds of people moved hurriedly about, tapping tablets in their hand, swiping screens on their phones, talking in frantic exchanges. Dozens of others studied screens on their desktops.

"What are we waiting for? Until we're all vaporized?" a uniformed man asked.

"Vaporized? Really?" a technician remarked from behind his computer screen.

"You know what I mean, damn it. We need to strike."

"Strike with what? Nukes?"

"If someone breaks into your house and points a gun at you, you don't just stare at them and wait for them to shoot you. You fight back. These — things — broke into our house and now we're just staring at them."

A newsflash exploded onto the screen. The Russians had attacked one of the towers very shortly after the structure had landed. They sent a squadron of fighter jets and their latest high-tech tanks to attack a tower outside of Moscow. Rough video footage of a tower being hit with intense gunfire filled the screen. Text scrolled across the screen beneath the video footage, the announcer extolling the news that a two hour barrage of constant gunfire and bombardment had cracked the base of the alien tower and sent the structure toppling over.

"Thank God for the Russians," somebody muttered. "Shoot first and ask questions later."

Across the world, jet fighters filled the skies, sending streams of rockets slamming into the towers. Massive tanks rumbled to nearly point blank range, barraging the towers in the heavily populated cities with heavy shells. Artillery bombarded the more remote towers from a distance.

They cheered and whistled and high-fived each other as screens filled with towers teetering, tumbling, and toppling.

"Whew," Jeremy said as he watched a tower in Chicago come crashing down on his monitor. "I really thought we were goners there for a while."

The corners of Bianca's wrinkles turned up. Jeremy smiled softly back. She really was beautiful when she smiled.

That's when Chuck charged into the room. "Stop!" He was a portly man with a full thick beard. His face was flushed a deep red and he was having trouble catching his breath. He hurried over to them and threw a jabbing finger at the display screens. "We have to get them to stop! Please, dear God, make them stop!"

Everyone looked at him, their faces still full of smiles, their voices still laced with joyous laughter.

"Relax, Chuck. It's over," Bianca said.

"Calm down, dude," Jeremy said.

"Take a chill pill, Chuck," someone else nearby said.

"You have to get them to stop! They all need to stop! Now!" Chuck raced to a computer and furiously tapped at the keyboard. He pointed to one of the large screens on a nearby wall. "We deciphered the greeting. We pulled out a visual, too."

Jeremy slowly looked away from Bianca and turned to Chuck. Rivulets of sweat trickled down the big man's forehead. "Chuck, really, you need to calm down."

"No, I don't. You all need to shut the fuck up and listen."

The screen spit static for a moment, then a figure appeared, a humanoid figure, but clearly an entity not from Earth. The entity had a large oval head with greenish-blue eyes that bore a close resemblance to the compound eyes of an insect. It had no nose, just several slits covered by membranes that puffed slightly in and out as it breathed. Its mouth was wide, its lips thick.

Everyone in the room went silent. Some mouths dropped open, but no words came out, no sounds. It was the first direct visual proof of life existing beyond their planet. It was a monumental moment, but no one had a single word to utter.

The entity spoke. "Greetings to the creatures of the third planet in the Sol system. Do not fear the towers. We are here to help you. We are the Delvaki of the Turon system. We too inhabit the third planet in our system. We share that cosmic unity.

"The Akanor are coming to your world. We sent you the towers to help defend your world against their attack. They need a few days to charge their shields after their long journey. Your strong sun will refuel their solar cells. So do not fear the sights and sounds you might see emanating from the towers.

"The Akanor will show you no mercy. You must be prepared."

Chuck pointed to the entity on the screen. "You gonna tell me to calm down again?"

Across the world, the cheering died and the whistling faded and the triumphant cries shriveled into silence. The attacks on the towers stopped, but most of them had already fallen. Ruins of the towers lay scattered across the planet.

Jeremy unbuttoned the third button on Bianca's blouse. They were in her downtown condo, the sun shining brightly through the large window that looked out on the city. His fingers trembled. She smelled delicious, like a soft scent of vanilla and lavender. It was very subtle, but it was there, a perfect combination of scents. He kissed her cleavage area and he heard her moan. He moved on to the next button, fumbling at it with his shaking fingers. He could see the slopes of her breasts, her erect nipples. He finished unbuttoning her blouse and parted the fabric to reveal her full breasts to his hungry gaze. He put his mouth to her nipple and gently sucked at it, licking the dark areola. She grabbed the back of his head and held him tight against her breast, pushing more of herself into his mouth.

Bianca reached down and rubbed her hand along his crotch, squeezing his manhood firmly. He moved up to her mouth and kissed her hard, thrusting his tongue into her mouth, tasting her. He slid his hand beneath her skirt, beneath her silk panties, and touched the curls of her womanhood. She shifted her legs, parting them further for him. He moved his fingers down, finding the wet folds that awaited their touch. He slid his finger into her wetness and she broke away from their kiss to moan hotly in his ear. He slid a second finger into her and she pulled herself tighter to him.

She pulled back and quickly unbuttoned his shirt. She peeled it off of him, tossing it the floor when she got it free of his arms. He removed her blouse in turn, tossing it next to his shirt.

Bianca grabbed at his jeans, unbuttoning them, unzipping them, tugging them down to his knees. She moved to the ground in front of him, taking his member into her mouth. He gasped with sheer pleasure at the warmth of her mouth on him. She cupped his balls and licked the underside of his shaft, running her tongue up and down his erection before taking it deep into her mouth again. He almost burst into her mouth.

Jeremy grabbed her and pulled her back up to kiss her again. She danced and wiggled out of her skirt and tugged her panties down to her ankles. He pulled away from the kiss to remove the rest of his clothing. She did the same. They stood naked in front of each other.

She grabbed his hand and pulled him over to the bed. They rolled on the silk sheets, hugging, touching, kissing, enjoying each other's bodies. Jeremy moved on top of her. He dipped down to kiss each of her breasts, rolling his tongue around her taut nipples.

Bianca reached down to grip his stiffness, guiding it towards her awaiting wetness. She put the tip of him into her and then released her grip. Jeremy could feel the warm heat of her on the tip of his manhood.

He reached down to kiss her and then plunged himself inside of her.

Outside, the sky filled with Akanor ships.

The world ended on Sunday.

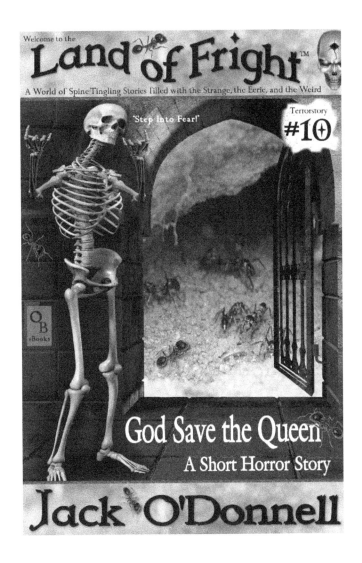

# TERRORSTORY #10
# GOD SAVE THE QUEEN

"**Kill the queen. That's all that matters.** After that, the entire colony will collapse and move on."

Jordan Trevane nodded. He fidgeted in the large office chair. He was a lanky young man with short brown hair. Dressed in faded blue jeans and a blue button collar shirt, he looked the part of a young professional computer technician, minus the pocket protector and corporate pens.

"You have to become the ant," Elias said.

"I'd like to cum on your aunt," Jordan said.

"Seriously?" Elias frowned as he adjusted his

157

glasses. Elias had a shadowy five-day growth of beard on his dark-skinned face. He had very short black hair, with tiny curls at the tips. His parents had come from Israel and he had a definitive Middle Eastern look to him.

Jordan nodded. "She's hot."

"Can you control yourself so we can get back to business now?"

"Sure. I got great self-control." Jordan spun a few circles in the office chair.

Elias studied the young man spinning in the chair before him. Jordan could be a little unwieldy at times, but damn if he didn't have some of the best dexterity he had ever seen. He could master any video game within a few hours. Give him a physical challenge and he'd nail the skill after a few tries. Just masterful hand-eye coordination. That was one of the primary reasons why he had been chosen to go first. Elias certainly hadn't chosen him because of his personality. Or his intelligence.

"Once you get inside, secrete a new pheromone. Make yourself a nest maintenance worker. You'll be able to move about freely without causing any alarm. Your size won't matter."

Jordan stopped spinning. "That's not what your aunt said."

Elias just kept going, ignoring Jordan's grin. "It's the pheromone scent that's the most important. Just make sure you secrete the right one."

"Secrete," Jordan said. "That's one of those nasty words like *moist*, isn't it?" He paused for a moment before repeating it. "Secrete."

"Once you find the queen, sec— spray the brood worker pheromone. That will let you get right up to her."

"Do you think she'll be happy to see me?"

Elias grit his teeth. "And then once you get to the queen, start doing some damage with those mandibles. Try not to kill any other ants if you can help it."

"Yeah, yeah. If I kill one it'll secrete a pheromone letting every other ant know it's dying and they'll come swarming in to see what the hell is going on. I know, I know. We went over this stuff a million times."

"Now it's a million and one," Elias said. "Remember, you need to kill the queen quickly and decisively."

Jordan nodded.

Elias grabbed a black helmet from the table nearby and handed it to Jordan. "Here. We adjusted the fit. Try it now." It looked pretty low tech for the high tech it contained. It looked somewhat like a football helmet, but instead of a face guard there was a curved screen. It was the screen where Jordan would be seeing the events unfold before him when Antee entered the nest. "No pressure, but you realize if this works, we will revolutionize pest control. We are all going to be filthy rich," Elias said.

"Me? I just like being filthy," Jordan said. "All over your aunt Carla." Jordan grinned and donned the helmet.

❧⟡❧

"Pre-launch checklist," Elias said. He spoke into the tiny mic attached to his headset.

"Pre-launch checklist," Jordan repeated. Jordan's

voice now came out of the speakers situated near the main viewing area, as well as into Elias's earpiece.

Elias sat at the main control panel station in front of a large screen, seeing what Jordan saw through his helmet visor. "Antennae."

"Tuned. I read you loud and clear." The antenna on the micro antbot moved up and down, back and forth. They were bent in the middle, curved just like the typical antennae of an ant in the wild.

"Mobility."

"Check."

Elias looked down to his left. The antbot was resting on a thin slide on the table nearby. He watched it crawl along the glass towards the edge of the slide. He looked back at the viewscreen. From the viewpoint of Antee, their ant microbot, the world looked staggeringly enormous. The edge of the slide looked like a giant curb of glass even though it was only millimeters tall.

He looked over to Jordan sitting in the control chair. The young man was suited up for a new kind of battle, wearing thin black gloves laced with sensors, the large helmet in place atop his head. Elias watched as Jordan wiggled his gloved fingers; each finger controlled one of Antee's legs. He was still amazed at the dexterity Jordan displayed. He could move each finger completely independently of the other. Elias had tried the gloves himself many times, but moving his middle finger always made his other fingers twitch. He had destroyed many micro antbots in his tests. It was an easy decision to count himself out for the first real test.

"Pheromone tanks," Elias said.

"The secret to ant communication," Jordan said in

a poor imitation of a science channel narrator. "Hey, how do you make a pheromone?"

Elias stared down at the tiny ant on the slide.

"Take away his pyramids."

Elias just blinked.

"C'mon, nothing?"

Elias could hear the frown in Jordan's voice. "Pheromone tanks," Elias repeated.

"Full and primed. Light is green. Forager scent. Check. Soldier scent. Check. Nest debris cleaner scent. Check. Brood worker. Check."

"Mandibles."

"Large and powerful for heavy lifting and defense."

Elias looked at the view screen, seeing the large mandibles open and close sideways like a pair of scissors. They were pretty damn formidable weapons, he had to admit. "Mandibles," he repeated.

"Check."

"Endoscopic front forward camera."

"All the better to see you with, my dear. Damn, you are ugly."

Elias glanced at the screen to see the profile of his face large on the screen. He pushed his glasses back up the bridge of his nose. "Endoscopic front forward camera," he repeated.

"Check."

"Endoscopic rear facing camera."

"All the better for you to get an ant's ass-view of the world." Jordan quickly added, "Check."

"Pre-launch checklist complete," Elias said.

They both were silent for a long moment.

"Let's go," Jordan finally said. "Bring me over there."

Elias looked down at the micro antbot. He stood up and moved over to the slide. He cautiously picked up the slide, making sure to hold it level. "Grab one of the apple pieces and lay a trail to the nest," he said into his mic.

"I'm telling you we should use grits instead," Jordan said. "They'll expand in those ant bellies and make them explode. My uncle Chapoor swears by it."

"That's an old wives' tale. It's not true. It doesn't work."

"You calling my uncle Chapoor an old wife? That's it. We're throwing down when this is over. The gloves are coming off and I'm coming after you."

Elias ignored his silly outburst. He walked over to the wall and stopped near the patio door that led outside. The ant colony was somewhere nearby, just beyond the threshold. They had observed ant activity in the house for several days before deciding the best area to launch the strike from. He lowered the slide to the ground, setting it down near several bits of apple pieces they had placed. "Just grab an apple piece. There's enough food there to keep them busy for hours."

"The only piece I want to grab—"

"I know. Is my aunt Carla." Elias gave a soft shake of his head. "Just grab an apple piece and spray a nice fat trail for other ants to follow. That much food will at least provide some distraction."

"Do ants have a big enough brain to actually get distracted?"

Elias didn't answer.

It was definitely a weird feeling, being so low to the ground, feeling so small, surrounded by everyday objects that seemed staggeringly massive. Jordan knew he was actually sitting in the control chair virtually piloting Antee, but he still felt like he was the ant. The helmet visor really immersed him into this new world.

He wiggled his fingers and the ant's legs moved. He trained vigorously to master the tiny robot's movement. Each leg was controlled by a finger, three on his left hand and three on his right, and he could move each leg independently of the other with ease and fine dexterity. Antee moved forward, heading toward a small crack in the floorboard that led to the large colony just outside the back door.

The slice of apple was now clutched in his mandibles. It was time to lay a forager success scent down. There was a tiny virtual control panel situated at the bottom of his vision. He glanced at the different scent icons. "Select food scent," he said. A food icon flashed to verify the found-food scent was selected. "Spray food scent." He didn't bother to look behind him; he knew Elias would see a green-colored trail being left behind him on the rear camera view screen. And sure enough Elias's voice came ringing into his helmet. "Food scent successfully deployed. Trail is being laid."

Laid. Why'd he have to say laid? His thoughts immediately went to Carla. Elias's aunt Carla. Her pretty little nose. Her sweet mouth. Her tight little body. Yeah, she was older. But so what? Carla was beautiful. He thought of taking Antee into her bedroom. He could just crawl up her bedpost, find the ideal spot above her bed, and watch her sleep.

Sleep? Hell, no. He'd watch her do much more than sleep. He'd watch her take her blouse off. He was certain she would be wearing a sexy lacy bra. She'd have a lovely deep line of cleavage, accenting her big breasts. Oh, yeah. She would slide her skirt off, wriggling that sweet ass of hers as she undressed, and he would be shocked to see that she wasn't wearing any panties at all. And she wouldn't be trimmed. Oh, no. She'd be full of hair. Dark black hair. All wild and unruly down there.

"Shit!"

The nervous shout of Elias's voice blasting through his helmet speakers brought Jordan out of his lusty reverie.

Another ant blocked his path. A large ant. A soldier ant. It flicked its antennae at him rapidly, circling him, touching its antenna to his antenna, brushing them against the head of his exoskeleton. Did it know something was not right about the Antee exoskeleton shell? At first, they were worried about the size of Antee. She was the size of a soldier ant, so she was larger than a typical worker ant. Would that be a tip off to the real ants? All of their preliminary tests showed that the pheromone scent was the most important part of recognition; the size of the exoskeleton didn't seem to matter as long as the proper scent was set down.

"Keep moving," Elias hissed into his ear. "Keep moving."

Jordan realized he had stopped Antee and immediately started moving her forward. The soldier circled him again, its large mandibles opening and closing in his rear-view camera as it rounded the antbot. But then the soldier moved on. It did not detect any imminent threat.

Jordan smiled.

How wrong that soldier ant was.

Everything glowed with a luminescent green. The night vision screen worked perfectly. There was movement everywhere. Dozens of smaller worker ants scurried about, some removing debris, others carrying food; many just scurried about doing whatever task they were bred to do to keep the nest at full operational capacity. It was funny, Jordan thought. He was just a tiny soldier ant, but he felt like a giant when he was surrounded by all the normal-sized worker ants. He saw one ant spit up a pool of water from its secondary social stomach, sharing it with its nest mates.

Numerous worker ants scurried up to him, waving their antennae around him, around the slice of apple in his mandibles. In his rear-view camera he saw dozens of them head off, following his trail that led to the treasure trove of apple bits they had scattered on the kitchen floor inside the house.

Jordan dropped the piece of apple from his mandibles and moved away from it. Several ants moved to the fallen apple piece. A few them crawled over it a few times, moving back and forth atop it. Then one of them picked it up, which was pretty impressive for such a small ant. The worker ant carried it deeper into a tunnel on his left. Jordan knew that led to a food storage chamber. There probably several other food chambers in various places throughout the nest. The other ants, the ones who had been inspecting the apple slice he had dropped, followed his food trail and headed out of the nest towards the kitchen.

Jordan immediately released a nest worker pheromone scent and moved Antee deeper into the colony. More ants scurried past him, paying him no heed. The walls of the tunnels the ants had carved out were incredibly smooth. For a brief moment, he paused to admire the craftsmanship of these little creatures, but then continued on deeper into the nest. He had a mission to accomplish. "I feel like a ninja," he muttered. "An ant ninja."

Jordan passed a pupa chamber and knew he was getting closer. Another ant approached him clutching a soft white body that looked like a worm with a small head. It was a larvae, the metamorphosis stage after the egg. The ant passed him, heading towards the pupa chamber. Another ant passed him, also carrying a white, wriggling larvae. He was definitely getting closer.

"I think it's time for the brood worker pheromone," Elias said in his ear.

Jordan glanced at the tiny virtual control panel situated at the bottom of his vision. "Select brood worker scent," he said in a quiet voice. A brood worker icon flashed to verify the selection. "Spray brood worker scent." He wasn't sure why, but he suddenly felt the need to whisper. "Brood worker scent deployed," he acknowledged in a soft voice after the deed was done. "Keep your voice down, will ya?" he said to Elias.

Jordan moved deeper into the nest.

And then Jordan saw her. The queen. She truly was a magnificent sight to behold, much larger than every other ant in the colony. In fact, she looked downright massive. She had her own chamber in the nest, an exclusive penthouse suite filled with adoring servants. He saw the visible stubs where her wings used to be, tell-tale protrusions on her thorax that were remnants of the wings the queen shed after her nuptial flight.

An egg spewed forth and a brood worker ant quickly grabbed it and took it away, making way for another egg to be laid. The brood worker ant cradled the egg in its mandibles and headed out of the queen's room, bringing the egg to the egg chamber to join its brothers and sisters. Hah, probably not brothers, Jordan corrected himself. Just sisters. All of the workers were females.

The queen's egg sac pulsated and throbbed. A fucking baby making machine in every sense of the word, he thought. He knew she could lay thousands of eggs a year.

Jordan moved slowly up to the queen ant. There were dozens of brood worker ants scurrying about, tending to the queen, cleaning her, feeding her. Something about her made him nervous. He felt like he was indeed in the presence of true royalty. He felt intimidated by her aura. There was a reverence to her that seemed to emanate from her entire body. Almost like a physical force.

"Wow."

Elias's voice coming through his helmet made him start. He had forgotten who he was for a moment, had forgotten Elias was even watching this with him. Being this close to the queen of the ants was mesmerizing.

"Don't just stand there. Do it," he heard Elias say.

Jordan moved forward, crawling up the queen's massive body with tentative steps, mingling with the other ants. He was the only soldier-size ant in the chamber but the other ants accepted his presence; the brood worker pheromone was doing its job. He could see the pulsing of the queen's womb as he moved up her large thorax.

That's when Jordan heard the voices. The tiny, tiny voices. Sounds of squealing and life. What the hell was that? They seemed to be coming from the eggs. No, not the eggs. From her womb. From the eggs yet to be laid. No, that was crazy. "Do you hear that?"

"Hear what?"

"Those voices. Those little voices."

"What? No," Elias said, dismissing his comment. "Come on, Jordan, do it. Quickly and decisively."

Jordan slowly eased the outer sheaths back from Antee's four forelegs, revealing the viciously sharp blades that lay hidden beneath. He opened his mandibles wide, pulling back the thin covering that had hidden brutally vicious serrated edges. He extended the hooked claws at the end of his legs, making them even longer and more cruelly curved.

The queen raised her head and looked directly at him. Jordan could feel the gaze of her many smaller eyes boring into him as her compound eyes locked onto him. It felt like thousands of eyes were physically gripping him. He felt frozen, unable to move.

"Fuck, Jordan, do it!"

Another voice came into Jordan's head. It wasn't the tiny voices. It wasn't Elias's voice. It was some other voice. A commanding voice.

And then the real attack began inside Jordan's head.

Detective Alistair Aldwich, middle name Arthur, stared down at the mutilated corpse. He preferred detective Aldwich, but just about everybody ended up calling him Triple A.

"Are those bug bites all over him?" Triple A heard a cop nearby ask.

Triple A looked down at the corpse. The guy's arms were peppered with red hot bumps and welts and thin scratches. His face had the same pattern of welts and nicks. A thicker red welt could be seen ringing the corpse's neck. "Could be. Looks like he got strangled first."

"Who is he?" another cop standing next to Triple A asked.

"Guy used to run this extermination company. Some newfangled hi-tech company. Nano-technology robots or some shit. Too bad. It was geared to really take off, they say." Triple A took a drag of his e-cigarette. A quick hit of cherry flavor filled his mouth. It helped mask the bitter taste he always got in his mouth at a murder scene. "Course that was before an employee went nuts and killed the boss. They're trying to find him. Some kid name Jordan Trevane." He shrugged. "So now who knows. It'll probably be just another failed start-up that collapsed."

The cop standing next to Triple A glanced at the large empty chair to his left, at the hi-tech array of equipment and screens on the table nearby, then looked back down at the body on the floor. "What was his name?"

Triple A stared down at the corpse at his feet. "Queen. Elias Queen."

# ABOUT JACK O'DONNELL

I'm having a lot of twisted fun exploring the Land of Fright™ and unearthing the stories I'm finding buried in those strange lands. I hope you are having some dark fun reading them.

Visit www.landoffright.com and subscribe to stay up-to-date on the latest new stories in the Land of Fright™ series of horror short stories.

Or visit my author page on Amazon at www.amazon.com/author/jodonnell to see the newest releases in the Land of Fright™ series.

Thanks for reading.

## - JACK

## MORE LAND OF FRIGHT™ COLLECTIONS ARE AVAILABLE NOW!

Turn the page and step into fear!

**Land of Fright™ terrorstories contained in Collection II:**

**#11 - Special Announcement**: A fraud investigator discovers the disturbing truth behind the messages on a community announcement board.

**#12 - Poisoned Land**: Savage hunters patrol the Poisoned Lands, demanding appeasement from the three survivors trapped in a surrounded building. How far will each one of them go to survive?

**#13 - Pool of Light**: A mysterious wave of dark energy from space washes over the Earth, trapping a woman and her friends in pools of light. Beyond the edges of the light, deep pockets of darkness hold much more than just empty blackness.

**#14 - Ghosts of Pompeii**: A woman on a tour of Italy with her son unwittingly awakens the ghosts of Pompeii.

**#15 - Sparklers**: A child's sparkler opens a doorway to another dimension and a father must enter it to save his family and his neighborhood from the ominous threat that lays beyond.

**#16 - The Grid**: An interstellar salvage crew activates a mysterious grid on an abandoned vessel floating in space, unleashing a deadly force.

**#17 - The Barn**: An empty barn beckons an amateur photographer to step through its dark entrance, whispering promises of a once-in-a-lifetime shoot.

**#18 - Sands of the Colosseum**: A businessman in Rome gets to experience the dream of a lifetime when he visits the great Colosseum — until he finds himself standing on the arena floor.

**#19 - Flipbook**: A man sees a dark future of his family in jeopardy when he watches the tiny animations of a flipbook play out in his hand.

**#20 - Day of the Hoppers**: Two boys flee for their lives when their friendly neighborhood grasshoppers turn into deadly projectiles.

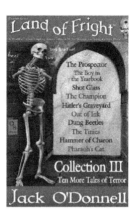

## Land of Fright™ terrorstories contained in Collection III:

**#21 - The Prospector**: In the 1800's, a lonely prospector finds the body parts of a woman as he pans for gold in the wilds of California.

**#22 - The Boy In The Yearbook**: Two middle-aged women are tormented by a mysterious photograph in their high school yearbook.

**#23 - Shot Glass**: A man discovers the shot glasses in his great-grandfather's collection can do much more than just hold a mouthful of liquor.

**#24 - The Champion**: An actor in a medieval renaissance re-enactment show becomes the unbeatable champion he has longed to be.

**#25 - Hitler's Graveyard**: American soldiers in WWII uncover a nefarious Nazi plan to resurrect their dead heroes so they can rejoin the war.

**#26 - Out of Ink**: Colonists on a remote planet resort to desperate measures to ward off an attack from wild alien animals.

**#27 - Dung Beetles**: Mutant dung beetles attack a family on a remote Pennsylvania highway. Yes, it's as disgusting as it sounds.

**#28 - The Tinies**: A beleaguered office worker encounters a strange alien armada in the sub-basement of his office building.

**#29 - Hammer of Charon**: In ancient Rome, it is the duty of a special man to make sure gravely wounded gladiators are given a quick death after a gladiator fight. He serves his position quietly with honor. Until they try to take his hammer away from him...

**#30 - Pharaoh's Cat**: In ancient Egypt, the pharaoh is dying. His trusted advisors want his favorite cat to be buried with him. The cat has other plans...

## Land of Fright™ terrorstories contained in Collection IV:

**#31 - The Throw-Aways**: A washed-up writer of action-adventure thrillers is menaced by the ghosts of the characters he has created.

**#32 - Everlasting Death**: The souls of the newly deceased take on solid form and the Earth fills with immovable statues of death...

**#33 - Bite the Bullet**: In the Wild West, a desperate outlaw clings to a bullet cursed by a Gypsy... because the bullet has his name on it.

**#34 - Road Rage**: A senseless accident on a rural highway sets off a frightening chain of events.

**#35 - The Controller**: A detective investigates a bank robbery that appears to have been carried out by a zombie.

**#36 - The Notebook**: An enchanted notebook helps a floundering author finish her story. But the unnatural fuel that stokes the power of the mysterious writing journal leads her down a disturbing path...

**#37 - The Candy Striper and the Captain**: American WWII soldiers in the Philippines scare superstitious enemy soldiers with corpses they dress up to look like vampire victims. The vampire bites might be fake, but what comes out of the jungle is not...

**#38 - Clothes Make the Man**: A young man steals a magical suit off of a corpse, hoping some of its power will rub off on him.

**#39 - Memory Market**: The cryptic process of memory storage in the human brain has been decoded and now memories are bought and sold in the memory market. But with every legitimate commercial endeavor there comes a black market, and the memory market is no exception...

**#40 - The Demon Who Ate Screams**: A young martial artist battles a vicious demon who feeds on the tormented screams and dying whimpers of his victims.

## Land of Fright™ terrorstories contained in Collection V:

**#41 - The Hatchlings**: A peaceful barbecue turns into an afternoon of terror for a suburban man when the charcoal briquets start to hatch!

**#42 - Virgin Sacrifice**: A professor of archaeology is determined to set the world right again using the ancient power of Aztec sacrifice rituals.

**#43 - Smog Monsters**: The heavily contaminated air in Beijing turns even deadlier when unearthly creatures form within the dense poison of its thick pollution.

**#44 - Benders of Space-Time**: A young interstellar traveler discovers the uncomfortable truth about the Benders, the creatures who power starships with their ability to fold space-time.

**#45 - The Picture**: A young soldier in World War II shows his fellow soldiers a picture of his beautiful fiancé during the lulls in battle. But this seemingly harmless gesture is far from innocent...

**#46 - Black Ice**: A vicious dragon is offered a great gift — a block of black ice to soothe the fire that burns its throat and roars in its belly. Too bad the dragon has never heard of a Trojan dwarf...

**#47 - Artist Alley**: At a comic book convention, a seedy comic book publisher sees himself depicted in a disturbing series of artist drawings.

**#48 - Dead Zone**: A yacht gets caught adrift in the dead zone in the Gulf of Mexico, trapped in an area of the sea that contains no life. What comes aboard the yacht from the depths of this dead zone in search of food cannot really be considered alive...

**#49 - Cemetery Dance**: A suicidal madman afraid to take his own life attempts to torment a devout Christian man into killing him.

**#50 - The King Who Owned the World**: A bored barbarian king demands he be brought a new challenger. But who can you find to battle a king who owns the world?

**Land of Fright™ terrorstories contained in Collection VI:**

**#51 - Zombie Carnival**: Two couples stumble upon a zombie-themed carnival and decide to join the fun.

**#52 - Going Green**: Drug runners trying to double cross their boss get a taste of strong voodoo magic.

**#53 - Message In A Bottle**: A bottle floats onto the beach of a private secluded island with an unnerving message trapped inside.

**#54 - The Chase**: In 18th century England, a desperate chase is on as a monstrous beast charges after a fleeing wagon, a wagon occupied by too many people...

**#55 - Who's Your Daddy?**: A lonely schoolteacher is disturbed by how much all of the students in her class look alike. A visit by a mysterious man sheds some light on the curious situation.

**#56 - Beheaded**: In 14th century England, a daughter vows revenge upon those who beheaded her father. She partners with a lascivious young warlock to restore her family's honor.

**#57 - Hold Your Breath**: A divorced mother of one confronts the horrible truth behind the myth of holding one's breath when driving past a cemetery.

**#58 - Viral**: What makes a civilization fall? Volcanoes, earthquakes, or other forces of nature? Barbarous invasions or assaults from hostile forces? Decline from within due to decadence and moral decay? Or could it be something more insidious?

**#59 - Top Secret**: A special forces agent confronts the villainous characters from his past, but discovers something even more dangerous. Trust.

**#60 - Immortals Must Die**: There is no more life force left in the universe. The attainment of immortality has depleted the world of available souls. So what do you do if you are desperate to have a child?

# AND LOOK FOR EVEN MORE LAND OF FRIGHT™ STORIES COMING SOON!

## THANKS AGAIN FOR READING.

Visit www.landoffright.com